DENNIS FRIEDMAN is a psychiat on phobias, sexual problems and c also the author of acclaimed books *History of the Royal Family; Darling* ......g *George V; Ladies of the Bedchamber: The Role of the Royal Mistress*; and *An Unsolicited Gift: Why We Do What We Do*. He is a Fellow of the Royal Society of Psychiatrists, has worked at St Bartholomew's Hospital, London, and was Medical Director of the Charter Clinic, London.

Acclaim for *Inheritance*

'An widely fascinating delve into the Windsors . . . compelling'
– Anne Edwards, author of *Matriarch*

Acclaim for *Ladies of the Bedchamber*

'It has been a great year for books about naughty ladies . . . I loved
Dennis Friedman's *Ladies of the Bedchamber.*'
– Edwina Currie, *New Statesman* Books of the Year, 2003

'A very good read, full of odd nuggets of fascinating information'
– *What's On In London*

Acclaim for *An Unsolicited Gift*

'Utterly fascinating' – Peter James, author of *Dead Man's Grip*

'Has kicked up a ruckus in Britain' – *Time* magazine

'Fascinating . . . maybe you are thinking: "Prince Charles – this
explains everything!"' – *The Australian*

THE LONELY HEARTS CLUB

Dennis Friedman

Peter Owen
London and Chicago

PETER OWEN PUBLISHERS
81 Ridge Road, London N8 9NP

Peter Owen books are distributed in the USA and Canada
by Independent Publishers Group/Trafalgar Square
814 North Franklin Street, Chicago, IL 60610, USA

First published in Great Britain 2012 by
Peter Owen Publishers

ISBN 978-0-7206-1489-3

A catalogue record for this book is available from the British Library.

Printed and bound by CPI Group
(UK) Ltd, Croydon, CR0 4YY

Thanks are due to my good friends Carlo, Howard, Jesus, Jonah, Keith, Louis, Peter, Roger and Vittorio, to my publisher and editor Antonia Owen, to my wife Rosemary and to Dr Malcolm Walker and Judith Walker for keeping the show on the road.

ONE

❦

The men in tracksuits and trainers stood in the late-summer sunshine in the street outside the gym wondering where to have lunch. Watching them from the doorway of his diner Franco hoped, as he did whenever he saw them, that they would patronize his café rather than any of the others in the area. His need for their custom was commercial. Theirs was esoteric. Coffee and sandwiches were much the same everywhere. Being able to sit and talk without feeling that they were in anyone's way fulfilled their lunchtime requirements.

'You can tell the time by them.' Franco addressed his only customer, an elderly woman in a cardigan with a button missing who was sitting in the corner. She was reading yesterday's *Metro* newspaper which someone had left on the table and didn't look up. Talking before breakfast was not what she had come for. She had spoken to order toast and a cup of tea. That was enough. Having to ask Franco to clear the mess left by the previous customer irritated her.

She would have sat elsewhere, but the other tables were equally messy. Franco knew he should have tidied the place up – and she knew she had chosen a café that had little going for it. Neither of them had met before, and they were unlikely to meet again. But for a moment Franco's apathy, combined with his customer's need for food, created a bond between them.

Franco liked to talk. The woman did not. She wished he would go away. She wasn't in the mood for conversation, but Franco would chat to anyone. It made the time go more quickly. Being on his own depressed him. He needed companionship. He was depressed before Val left him, but having no one to talk to made the fact that he was on his own worse. Since the divorce he had neglected his business. A glance through the open door put most customers off. He neglected himself as well as the café and looked as if he hadn't long got out of bed. There were little tufts of hair on his chin, and there was garlic on his breath. The customers didn't care for his proximity. The expression 'in your face' came to mind; not a particularly agreeable one.

It cheered him up when people chatted to him. He hoped the men from the gym would arrive soon and lighten the atmosphere. They brought with them a friendly chaos. It didn't occur to him that their vivaciousness might conceal a sense of futility and that their mildly manic behaviour might cover up unresolved problems or that they might need him as much as he needed them. He couldn't have known that dumping their gear on the floor of his café might reflect something within themselves they might want to abandon. Had his thinking been more reflective he would have realized that the men from the gym had chosen his café because its chaos echoed their inner conflicts and for a time offered relief from them. But what only they could know was that whatever negative feelings they may have brought with them that morning disappeared when they were together.

Their frequent visits served only to convince Franco that other customers might also feel at home in casually carefree surroundings, despite knowing that even if passers-by glanced in they usually carried on walking. He had also misread the behaviour of the gym group. They did not, in fact, like chaos but were doing their best to rid themselves of a lifetime of clutter and found in Franco's café a welcoming refuse bin. Franco was adept

8

at misreading what went on around him. Despite his wife telling him that one of the reasons she was leaving him was because he not only looked a mess but was a mess, he had continued to believe she wasn't serious. The woman at the corner table reminded him of Val. Familiar feelings of guilt swept over him. He reached for a paper towel from behind the counter, wet it in the sink next to the coffee machine and half-heartedly swabbed the round table by the window.

'I don't need this,' he volunteered, but his solitary customer pretended not to hear him. It was Val he was really talking to. The cardigan lady decided that next time she wanted a cup of tea she would go elsewhere or, better still, make sure she always had milk in her fridge.

The men in tracksuits and trainers invariably chose the round table. Although it was virtually identical to the others they told him that they preferred that one because of the view. He hadn't noticed that there was a view, only a never-ending cavalcade of tourists making their way to the nearby museum. Perhaps that was what they meant. He wasn't interested in passers-by or in any other form of continuity. He was interested only in those who came in and bought something – even if it was only a sandwich – and then left.

He looked away for a second. A moment before the room had been empty, and suddenly they were there. How could he not have noticed them? Val was right. She used to tell him that he never noticed anything. Noisy and friendly, they brought in what he thought of as a continental atmosphere. Taking chairs from other tables so that they could sit together, they dumped their fleece jackets and gym gear on the floor, shut the door because it was draughty and in no time were responsible for a comfortable disorder. More than once he had told them that the door had to remain open because there were no windows in the little room

9

which had once been a tobacconist's. It had a fixed window only and a door with a now long-gone fanlight.

No sooner had Franco opened the door again than the jolly overweight foreign man got up and shut it. A pal down the road had told him that the gym guys used to come to her place, but when she insisted that her door be kept open for the same reason they left and never came back. Pocketing the coins the elderly lady had left on the table Franco shrugged and decided to put up with it. They brought in chaos, but at least it was cheerful chaos. He liked it, even when a couple of them called out in Italian how they wanted their coffee. Franco didn't speak Italian, but they assumed he was Italian because of his name. His name was Frank. Franco sounded better in the same way that panini sounded better than bread. What they brought in was an existential confusion that had coloured their lives, distorted their relationships and eroded their talents.

Knowing only that they were from the gym across the road, he tried while he was busy behind the counter to discover more about them. Their habits never varied. One always sent his coffee back because it was cold; another insisted on picking up the tab; an older one continually asked questions; another brought his own flask for the coffee and occasionally ordered a slice of brown bread which he thought came with the coffee, like milk or sugar. The short fat one might have worked in a restaurant because he always insisted on carrying the tray to the table and, when Franco was busy, would stand behind the counter and help him butter the bagels. Occasionally a weirdo would accompany them. Quieter than the others, he looked perpetually worried. Although Franco might have recognized them anywhere he couldn't recognize the personality traits that made them what they were.

While he was dealing with their order he could hear them mulling over something they had been discussing earlier and their need to find answers. But no matter how often they came to his café he had never once noticed in detail their interactions with each other.

He pretended not to listen. He liked their noisy discussions although he wasn't sure what they were going on about. It gave his little café a sophisticated air, to which passers-by might be attracted. Those who paused to look at the menu, fixed to the inside of the shop window with tape, might think of it as a place in which to be seen, a place frequented by intellectuals. He rather regretted the smoking ban, because a smoke-filled room had a Dickensian feel to it which he thought Americans, with their passion for a remote past which as a nation had been denied them, might find attractive.

He was slicing some ham that he had taken out of the freezer and smelling it to check whether it had gone off, when one of the group stood up. 'I've got to go,' he announced. Picking up their gear, they left together. For the first time Franco was struck by how close they seemed. What one did they all did. They arrived together, talked together and left together. He could see them walking down the street still talking and then standing for a while and finally disappearing altogether.

TWO

✢

The group, outwardly noisy but inwardly thoughtful, enjoyed their twice-weekly gym session which had, over time, evolved into an emotional as well as a physical work-out. All in very late middle age they had been told by their cardiologists that supervised exercise, following heart surgery, improved life expectancy. By working out regularly, with no ill effects, they were able to convince themselves that their health problems were behind them. Only recently had they realized they attended the gym regularly not so much for the exercise but because they felt at one with each other. Why this intimacy had come about they were unable to explain and often discussed the matter after their exercise session, either in the gym's canteen, in Franco's while having a sandwich or over a celebratory birthday lunch. Their closeness went far beyond their heart problems. It was based on something vaguely familiar. Whether it had to do with all being in the same boat as far as their health was concerned, they didn't know. But it puzzled them. Even their conversation, personal, political, academic or simply banter, worked better when whatever they spoke of was thrown open to them all. They felt they were all of a piece. Should two of them momentarily split off from the others and exchange intimacies, if only briefly, the others would feel left out.

It was not mentioned and didn't need to be, but it was concern for the other which drove the group's thinking. Idle gossip about the buses or the weather, which were taking place around them, had no place in their thoughts. Anonymity was important. Surnames weren't exchanged. In their tracksuits and their trainers they were barely distinguishable one from the other. No effort was made to enquire into anyone's religious, financial, social or marital status. Neither were they interested in one another's ages, which varied from forty to eighty. What they saw was what they got, and what they got was what they wanted. They were comfortable together, and if occasionally one or other of them was reminded of someone familiar from the past it was not commented on.

None of them was in a hurry to return to his life outside the gym where they would revert to how others saw them rather than how they saw themselves. In their twice-weekly sessions nothing was expected of them. Knowing nothing of the other allowed them to see in him whatever they wanted to see as well as the freedom to be whatever or whomever they wished.

What was obvious, although not to Franco or to the others at the gym, was that they exchanged views about everything, were free to express them and always found in each other an interested and responsive audience.

Despite the fact that they shared heart problems health was rarely discussed, finding the illusion of immortality far more attractive. Although heart to hearts were frequently on the agenda, the heart as a pump was definitely not. Perhaps what united them was incongruity rather than harmony, difference rather than similarity or curiosity rather than knowledge, but while they existed as a vibrant, lively and thoughtful group, when they split up it was as if they ceased to exist. Out of sight was out of mind. In the early days it was only when they were at the gym that they shared their thoughts and feelings. It was months, years even, before some of them became aware of who the other was, where he lived or what he did when he was out of sight. If they thought about it at all they realized that they neither needed nor wanted to know. Their existence as a group was enough.

They wondered whether this was beginning to change. Was it the sandwich at Franco's or the social activities in which they were gradually becoming involved that were bridging the gap between their existence in the gym and the realities of everyday life? They liked Franco's but wondered sometimes about the effects socializing in his café might have on their experience of one another. The diner was never busy, and in it they felt carefree and at home – probably because they were not at home. The 'special' was the same every day, and they didn't enquire about it. What they had really come for had more to do with their thoughts than the food. They were hungry for information. Chatting among themselves at Franco's, they waited for their orders as a theatre audience might wait for the drama to begin.

THREE

Benedict Fanshawe, a retired church architect, had achieved fame among his contemporaries by designing a swimming-pool in a well-known gentlemen's club that wouldn't have looked out of place in a cathedral. He was reserved, modest and diffident in manner, although not averse to the occasional cutting comment disguised as humour when he thought he could get away with it. The conversion of abandoned churches into sports centres for the disabled, another of his interests, allowed him to think about the link between restoration and religion. He believed that managing disability through exercise, within the 'reach for the heavens' steepled design of the church, was an interface between physical activity and faith. Being good, looking good and feeling good, he thought, were keys to harmony. His concern for others was in direct proportion to his perception of their concern for him. He regarded such an interaction not as cynical but as an important cohesive ingredient for the survival of communities. He had wondered for some time whether that also applied to the survival of their group.

He was occasionally referred to as the Ancient Mariner, an appellation that someone had attached to him for reasons none of them could remember. Benedict privately took it as a vague reference to the wisdom that they assumed had come to him with age rather than their need for someone dependable to steer their boat.

He acknowledged that he liked looking at the sea and often saw himself as the group's helmsman, someone responsible for guiding them through waters as yet uncharted. But he also hated getting wet. Talking about issues or designing a pool was one thing, but getting one's hands dirty (or wet) was another. But no one could argue with the idea that life was a journey. Neither could anyone have any more idea than he about where they were going. What was increasingly clear was that they were all happy to be involved in a game of intellectual tennis – batting ideas back and forth, not so much to score points but because by putting the ball in someone else's court views could be exchanged about what life and, particularly, their lives might be about.

Benedict's studied manner was intended to suggest to the others that he would be the most likely of all to help interpret patterns of behaviour which might shed light not only on who they were but why they were. He was happy to play that role. He had, however, one unspoken proviso: he made it clear that he didn't wish to be referred to as Ben but as Benedict.

He was probably the most articulate of them all and ascribed this to information gleaned from listening daily to the BBC Radio 4's current affairs *Today* programme while having breakfast and comparing it with the Yesterday channel he viewed as an unintended horror version of *Today*. Did remembering the past discourage people from repeating it? And, if it didn't – which was fairly obvious to anyone witnessing tribal violence – what was the point of psychotherapy which depended on helping the unhappy rid themselves of their anxieties by encouraging them to recall what had led them to be worried in the first place? If why you are is so important, why did he not benefit from being introduced to why he was when he was having therapy? His therapist might have had several 'eureka' moments, but Benedict couldn't remember having any. Perhaps it was having someone listen that was therapeutic. The group listened and seemed to like him. He couldn't think what else it did, but he felt a lot happier for being part of it.

There was something that he wanted the group to hear about. It had to do with why he had never married. One day he would bring it up. It seemed too personal for the moment. He wasn't sure how the others might feel. It would keep. He went over it in his mind, wondering also whether he was becoming too preoccupied with God by working in churches, albeit mainly abandoned ones, particularly since he had always thought of himself, intellectually at least, as an atheist. The idea that God might exist, in the heavens or in the Church or somewhere as yet unknown, was something to which he had been giving increasing thought. It must be something to do with the people he was associating with in church. It wasn't so much what God the Father expected of him, he told himself, but what his own father had expected of him during his childhood that really troubled him.

He had long since taken the view that God was another term for conscience. If your conscience accepted that what you were doing was OK, then it was OK. But if your conscience had become condemnatory, then what? It seemed perfectly obvious to him that if his conscience was giving him a hard time it was because he had provoked it by behaving badly. Confession and repentance were said to be remedies for guilt. Remorse and atonement were two more. There were some – he shuddered as he thought of it – who practised self-flagellation, either mental or physical. He had disapproved of corporal punishment since being beaten at school for failing to do his homework. He was going to think hard before he asked the group for its views on what he might be doing wrong at the moment.

Current affairs had become his homework. It ensured that

17

he was never short of something to talk about, to expand on and to impress the others who admired his knowledge of what was and might be. He decided against telling them where some of it came from. He was not yet ready for any form of revelation. One morning at coffee time, brushing back his long greying hair over his ears, he began acting out the role which he sensed they expected of him. Despite no one having asked him he said, 'It's a pilgrimage.'

No one felt the need to ask Benedict what he meant. They knew. They just looked interested and waited to hear the views of someone who knew as little about life's journey as they did.

'Not to Canterbury or Mecca or Jerusalem but to Lourdes. We all think we've got something wrong with us and need someone to fix it. Not a physical fix,' he added. 'We know all about stents and pacemakers. It's more likely to be an emotional fix or possibly a religious one.' He put on what he thought of as his mystic look and continued, 'Life might even be a journey of our imagination. Perhaps it exists only when we talk about it.'

He looked at the others to make sure they were listening and then paused because he was thinking of himself. He was the one with psychological problems. All the others seemed quite happy.

He sipped his coffee to give him time to think about what he had said. He accepted that he was stretching his existential fantasies a bit far, but to his surprise he was drawn to the spiritual feel of it. He felt his mood lifting. Perhaps it was the caffeine or thinking of the stained-glass windows and angels in a church he was restoring, or maybe it was because he was stimulated by the group's interest in what he was telling them. Whether they were cheered by what he had said he had no idea, but the notion of someone listening to him always made him feel good. Being ignored made him miserable. Dragging himself back from memories of a deaf mother whom he had believed as a child had never listened to him, because, he later discovered, she couldn't hear him, made him wish that his father had told him about her deafness before it had been too late to prevent him from losing his faith in women in general.

There was a thoughtful silence while the group reflected on what Benedict had said. The fact that their fate might lie in the hands of a higher being had made them, as well as Benedict – despite his at best intermittent spirituality – vaguely uneasy. They might have felt even more ill at ease if they had known that he was lost in 'if onlies' and had forgotten what he was going to say. But they all knew what the journey was. They were on it, but so was everyone. It was hardly worth talking about. Nevertheless they wanted to talk about it.

Drago Pavlovic, permanently unemployed, was thought by the others to have once been a waiter in his native Croatia, a view with which his deeply lined intellectual features seemed at variance. He was known for his rare but considered comments. In a quiet and sometimes hard-to-understand Dalmatian accent he said, 'Maybe we are on a bus and we do not get off.' He paused for a moment to wonder if he was expressing himself correctly. 'There is perhaps not a bus stop.'

A lifelong commitment, an unbroken journey, a total dependency on someone in charge, whether benevolent or other-wise, particularly if no one has any say in the matter, turned on a verbal tap. It didn't appeal to any of them. They began to speak about being controlled, at first by bus drivers then by their wives and then, perhaps not surprisingly since insight was a theme in most of their discussions, by their pasts.

Jerry Nickerson, a retired detective superintendent with a booming voice, a piercing look and an overwhelming conviction that he was right about most things, still looked the overweight policeman he had once been. No one quite knew how to take him, particularly since he had been seen one morning being dropped off at the gym by an attractive woman driving an expensive car. Nicknamed Nickers by a possibly paedophilic PE instructor at his boarding-school, a pseudonym which throughout his adolescence he had tried unsuccessfully to shrug off, he was regarded by the rest of them – possibly rightly – as something of an expert on getting to the bottom of things.

'A genuinely concerned bus driver would open the door to let someone off even if there wasn't a bus stop,' he told them in a gravelly tone honed by years of authoritarian misuse and alcohol abuse. It was a voice they had all become used to and had turned up their own volume to match it. 'But a bus driver with an inflexible attitude to his job and to the needs of others could deny them their right to choose their destiny if he wanted to.'

Drago looked puzzled. Had his English let him down? 'Do you mean destination?' he asked. What a language! There were too many words all for the same thing. He would never learn to speak it like the others.

Jerry knew that Drago was thinking of journey's end for the bus driver and his passengers, but what he was musing about was his controlling mother and the effect she'd had on him as a child and was probably still having – not on his destination but on his destiny. He wanted to explain to Drago why he actually did mean destiny, but he couldn't bring himself to talk to the others about his childhood right then. He didn't want to think about the north-London suburb in which he had been brought up and the problems he'd had with his social-climbing parents. He was still embarrassed, even after so many years, that he had been brought up by a nanny. He didn't want his friends to judge him on his background, privileged in one way but awful in others. He shifted uneasily on his chair and wondered whether it was only over-weight people who had weighty thoughts. He would have liked to have changed the subject; he preferred the idea of discussing ponderous subjects. He would have to save it for another time.

He knew that they were waiting to hear his views on life's journey, but he was still thinking about his nanny. In the first place he thought it unlikely that any of them would have had one. He frowned because he felt he was being patronizing. He wanted to feel at one with them; not look down on them. He would have to add it to his weighty thoughts list. He wouldn't have minded if he'd had a nanny because his mother had a job to go to or even because she was pretending to be something she was not. Either option might have been acceptable or at least understandable. But he knew the real reason was that where they lived it was customary to employ one and that his mother had to keep up with all the other middle-class parents in their apartment building. He thought of them now as being not so much upwardly mobile as upwardly pretentious. His parents could afford a nanny, and that was that. He realized that he was being unkind because he had forgotten about his younger sister. She had definitely needed one. Running a close second to what he felt about nannies he reminded himself that he didn't like his sister either, although seeing him waiting at the bus stop the week before she had given him a lift to the gym.

There was something else about nannies that concerned him. Having one was only one of his mother's failings. She had also owed him a personal duty of care which she had failed to deliver. Playing bridge every afternoon with her friends at her club instead of playing Happy Families every afternoon with him at home had given playing a meaning far removed from the one to which he had been entitled. He was eight when his parents split up. It was ironic that it was his nanny who had to tell him that his mother had been having fun and games somewhere else. If he had not had a nanny his mother would have looked after him and there would have been no time for fun and games else-where. It had to be elsewhere, because as far as he could

21

remember she had never had fun and games with him. If she had, she wouldn't have needed to go to the bridge club for it. He paused in his thinking to tell himself not to be so fanciful. But he had still not forgiven her for failing to give him what he believed, as her first-born child, she owed him. It was a debt she had never paid. It's not that the world owes me a living, he told himself – but his mother's legacy would have been of more use to him if what she had left him hadn't consisted almost entirely of a life-long need for approval.

No one, not Drago nor anyone else, would believe that his mother, like the bus driver, had denied him the right to choose where he wanted to go, although she was certainly good at telling him where he could get off. He smiled fleetingly. He would have liked to have shared that play on words with the others but couldn't bring himself to talk about his mother as a bus driver with little concern for passengers, since he had been one of them himself. Even thinking about it made him angry. What made him angrier was that for reasons that had more to do with his prudish outlook on life and despite the sometimes bizarre sexual fantasies that had occupied much of his thinking as an adult, he hadn't looked to other women to compensate for what he had missed out on as a child. Unlike his mother and many others whose paths had crossed his during his working life, he had never played away from home. In his more thoughtful moments he realized that seeking reassurances that he was lovable from one woman after another might have had its moments, but in the long run his need for input had instead turned him from becoming a sex addict to a thirst at first for alcohol and then, later, for knowledge. He had turned into an encyclopaedia.

Lost in musings about hating card games and hating tabloid English – like the expression 'playing away from home' – and with the happy realization that he had found a collection of people who liked playing grown-up Happy Families, he could just make out a background conversational buzz. He tuned into what his friends were saying. They had given up waiting for him to give them his views on life's journey and edged sideways into talking about authority.

While none of them liked the idea of being controlled, Harold Andrews, a retired pharmacist who had given them the impression that he had been an Oxford don and who had lately told them that his expertise lay in tapestry, was suggesting that ultimately they had no say in their choice of destination or of their destiny. Harold, who usually said very little while always looking interested in what others were talking about, glanced around the room while he gathered his thoughts. He didn't want to be overheard, although he knew what he was about to say could hardly be considered confidential. Still, he told himself, you never know what could slip out. But, apart from Franco, who was speaking on his mobile with his back turned, the room was empty. Franco didn't count. They assumed that he wouldn't understand what they were saying despite the fact that he was speaking English into his phone.

'Most parents used to bring up their children to be obedient,' Harold said, having satisfied himself that only the group was listening.

'When I was growing up "disobedient" was a frightening word. It meant that something awful was about to happen to you. I had to deal with that threat on my own. I had no ally in my so-called nursery. You forget how helpless you are as an only child. Nothing much ever happened to me, but I'm sure that my attitude to authority now was determined by how often the word "obedient" was misused in my childhood. "Obey" must be one of the worst words in the English language. Look at how many people got away with murder during the Second World War on the grounds that they were just obeying orders.'

He was suddenly reminded of his bullying father whose sole ambition, in retrospect, seemed to be his oft-stated wish 'to make a man of him'. Harold felt a shockwave hit him somewhere in his chest. He wondered if he was having a heart attack. It really shook him up to the extent that he stopped speaking. He wasn't even listening to what Jerry was saying. Why had he never reminded himself of his father's attitude before? He must have blanked it out. As a child, being made a man seemed a punishment. He had never wanted to be made a man. He was shaking. He stood up and then sat down again, muttering something about the chair being uncomfortable.

Jerry wondered what was wrong with Harold. It would probably be better not to embarrass him by asking. Jerry had his own problems. What would they think of a retired senior police officer who was still struggling with feelings of being abandoned as a child by the one person he needed more than anyone else? The last thing he wanted to talk about was that he had missed out on something vital to his well-being caused by his absentee mother. He thought he could understand how Harold might be feeling about being told what to do or whatever it was that had upset him. But Jerry liked the idea of discussing authority. That was something that he didn't mind talking about. Authority was one of his pet likes – probably, he thought, because he had never really had it.

'I do not believe in blind obedience,' he said to Harold, realizing this sounded rather pompous but hoping that it might help Harold take his mind off whatever was bothering him. Harold pretended to listen, but he was too preoccupied to take in what Jerry was saying.

Benedict was thinking that nothing was just black or white. There were times to obey orders as well as times not to, but he decided not to say so, although Jerry seemed to sense what he was thinking. Benedict's face had a disapproving look.

'Actually I'm rather fond of authority,' Jerry went on, hoping to placate Benedict. 'One of the reasons I joined the police force was because I like being in charge. Police authority is never blind, you know. There are rules, but they are sensible ones. The good thing about it is that the higher up the ladder you go there are more people below you to boss around than there are above you telling you what to do.' Jerry stopped for a moment because he thought what he had said sounded a bit obvious and, moreover, did not show him in a particularly good light. No one seemed to have noticed, so he carried on. 'They had to do whatever I told them. Another reason why I worked so hard was because I wanted to be in control. I loved saying "It's an order!" but I never abused my power. The rules would never allow for that,' he said after reflecting for a moment and wondering whether he was sounding more than a little hypocritical. 'Making enquiries and a need to have a say in a matter and being listened to was great. I had missed out on all that while I was growing up. My parents hadn't the slightest idea of my needs. They probably thought I didn't have any. They never asked me about them, but they were always giving me instructions. I can't remember what my mother used to tell me to do – probably tidy my room or something – but when my father told me to do something I always challenged it.'

He wondered why he was talking as if his mother had actually featured in his childhood when he knew she had not. He knew why. He wanted to be the same as the others. He was looking for acceptance. He smiled. 'I made up for that at work by telling everyone else what to do. They never questioned anything. They weren't allowed to.'

Luc Labue, former owner of two gastropubs in London's docklands, said, 'Children need to be told what to do when they are young, otherwise they don't know what to do when they are older. Benjamin, the baby of our family, he's a criminal. He's always attacking the police. Maybe my father wasn't strict enough. I don't know. Maybe he was too strict. Anyway he's in prison now.' He shrugged. He looked as if he would have liked to have shrugged off what he had just said.

Everyone smiled sympathetically, but Luc shifted uncomfortably on his chair. He kicked the leg of the table. He wanted to kick himself for telling them something of which he was ashamed. He decided to say nothing for a while. Perhaps they would forget that he had said it.

Jerry thought that Luc's father had probably been *too* strict if his son had grown up wanting to have a go at authority all the time, but he didn't say so because he – and probably some of the others – sensed that Luc had regretted telling them about his antisocial brother. Jerry's father wasn't strict; he was simply incomprehensible. The child's need to know had begun early. He had never forgotten that as soon as he could speak he would ask his father questions, the answers to which invariably puzzled him. He had rather liked his father who, unlike his mother, had at least lived in the same house as he did. 'I didn't feel I was talking out of turn with my father. I always asked "Why?" when I was told to do something. Whoever was looking after me at the time would just say "Do as you're told!", but my father would tell me that Y was a crooked letter. He said it like it was important, like it was something I should know – something I should never forget. I used to wonder whether it was one of his jokes. He often laughed while he was telling me. I have always remembered it, as it happens, but I had no idea at the time what he was talking about. I must have been about twelve before I could distinguish between the letter Y and the word "why". The one good thing that came out of it was that I was more or less forced by his inability to give me straight answers to try to find things out for myself whenever I needed to know something.'

He regarded the others and hoped they didn't think that he was running his father down. Regardless of what he had just said, he had appreciated his father's parental involvement despite believing that it might have been more than a little misguided. There was an upside to it. It had been helpful in his choice of career. It had just struck him that had it not been for his father's irritating responses to his questions as a child he might have chosen a career more suited to his genuine need for information. He was intrigued by that thought. He might have become a research scientist instead of a policeman and discovered a cure for something horribly malignant. But what if the malignancy to which he would have dedicated his life to eradicating turned out to be absentee mothers? Would that have been more acceptable than re-enacting the effect his father had upon him? He wondered whether a detective in the police force made a greater or lesser impact on society than an oncologist. Crime and cancer were both malignancies that eat away at people's well-being. Perhaps it would not have mattered what choice he had made.

It wasn't until he had become an adult that he thought he understood why his father had been so reluctant to disclose any kind of information – whether to him or, probably, to anyone else. He thought it must have been based on a fear of talking out of turn, a hangover from a Victorian upbringing with his own strict father. He remembered being pleased to have found an explanation that might in time allow him to wipe clean the slate on which the memories of his father had been recorded.

'No one arrives in adult life as a blank canvas on which they can paint whatever they want on to it,' he said eventually. 'We all end up with a canvas that has something on it already. Whether what's on it come from the way we were treated or caused by chance events while we were growing up or by our genes I have no idea. All we can hope is that we find something useful to do with it.'

His friends made noises of agreement. But it was Harold, tall, ungainly and invariably anxious-looking, who had been on the conversational fringe of the group for a while who seemed to be tuned into Jerry's several dilemmas. After all, it had only been that morning that he had mentioned something to the effect that not only was he a retired academic but that his major interest was medieval French tapestry.

In a rare moment of thinking totally divorced from his occasional non-worldly comments on topics that usually baffled most of them – and having more or less got over recalling his father's wish to make a man of him – Harold said, 'I don't believe in nannies. They get in the way. Mothers with talent and ambition make their contribution to the next generation's gene pool by staying at home and having more babies. They go back to work and do a job which could just as well be done by a man.'

There was a metaphorical drawing in of breath as the others reflected on a side to Harold they had not previously considered. Even he seemed surprised by his suggestion that women should not only forego their careers to bring up babies but have more of them. He quickly withdrew into his more usual habit of looking interested but saying little, although not before noting that, although everyone had affected a liberal attitude regarding women's rights, they were not nearly as put out by what he had said as he thought most women would have been.

Jerry, in particular, felt an immediate affinity with Harold. Agreeing with someone was not something that sat comfortably with him, but his experience of mothering could hardly have encouraged him to another conclusion. 'Bringing up someone else's baby can't be right,' he said with feeling. 'It's still practised by the royals. It was tried in the kibbutzes. It's like Communism. Social systems may sound good on paper, but they seldom work because the family is more important than the state. Stalin and other autocrats may have thought the opposite was true, but no one else did.' Except neglectful mothers, he thought, but didn't say so.

Harold also found an ally in Benedict. 'Look at all the men who claimed to be fathers of their people –from Abraham to Mao or from Jesus to Mohammed. The population is expected to bond with them instead of with their actual parents. As an alternative to sibling rivalry with kids fighting you have tribal rivalry with everyone fighting.' Warming to his theme, he added, 'The Pope even translates as Il Papa in Italian. It's like Catholic priests being called Father and Anglican priests Vicar. All vicarious parents should be banned, including nannies. Come to think of it, deputies of any description are never popular. No one really wants to see the locum when the GP's on holiday.'

None of them disagreed with this. Their involvement with pills and reassurance required an interested third party's bonding with them to keep them going. Hoping the stand-in would intuit what would allow them to leave the primary-care clinic feeling better than when they had entered it ten minutes earlier was something understood only by their regular confidant. Ten minutes' satisfaction and twenty minutes waiting to obtain it seemed to both doctor and patient a more or less exact reflection of what they had been brought up to expect from life, from breastfeeding onwards.

'It's always been men who've insisted on running things,' Benedict contributed. 'It's true that there has been the occasional female in charge: Margaret Thatcher, Golda Meir, Mrs Bandaranaike and Angela Merkel and,' after a mischievous glance around to ensure that no one would be offended, 'the odd Queen here and there. And the Church is gradually recognizing women. But in the past it's been men who have been in the top jobs. Where did they think women were all the time? They assumed they were at home having babies and looking after them. Progressive thinkers like we are – male of course – still think like that.'

None of them thought for a moment that their thinking was progressive but didn't argue with Benedict's tongue-in-cheek assessment of it, nor did it take long for them to agree with him, despite having previously given the subject little thought. They were pleased to accept that that was how people saw them.

Jerry knew that with the possible exception of Benedict, who seemed more concerned with the role of fathers, they were getting carried away with their revised thinking on the role of women in society. 'Of course women should have careers if that's what they want. They should make their contribution but also be given properly paid down-time to bond with their babies.' As an after-thought he added rather irritably, 'If they really want to be as men obviously they can't have babies. But they can still play a maternal role. Women staying at home and managing infants is a waste of their talents when they could be in Number 10 managing the nation. A woman's hand at the tiller might just be what everyone needs. Men may have been given a free hand, but they have never played their cards right. They've not done a brilliant job. The only problem is that once someone's in power – whether male or female – they are seldom satisfied. The have-nots have nothing and want everything, and the haves have everything and want more of it.'

A woman was certainly what he had needed. The 'locum' had never done him much good. He wanted the real thing. Unfortunately women couldn't be in two places at once, he thought, despite their claim to be better at multi-tasking than men.

Silas Welch was always quiet and thought by the others to be depressed for reasons that he had not disclosed. He had reluctantly admitted to being a sculptor but told them he was thinking of giving it up for something else. He spoke out of the blue, because he was often silent for long periods. No one quite saw the connection to what had come before. 'For the first time in my life I feel that my parents, who died when I was very young, disappeared before they had a chance to fuck me up. It is very odd after all these years of self-pity suddenly to feel rather lucky . . .' He wondered why he had said this, because he knew it not to be strictly accurate. His father may have disappeared before he was born, but his mother had remained a thorn in his side until he had grown up and left home. It must have been wishful thinking – perhaps combined with a desire to impress them with his knowledge of poetry. He would have liked a nanny. Anything would have been better than being self-raising. He smiled and for the remainder of the morning felt rather better. He could have said that he could have grown up to be a loaf of bread and made them laugh but decided against it because he wanted them instead to puzzle over what he had said in self-conscious reference to Philip Larkin.

Luc thought he spoke for everyone when, after being silent after telling them that his brother was in prison, said, 'I think we are like this because of how they bring us up. My mother always said he is like this because of how she brought him up.' He turned to Harold. 'Are you saying that we'd have been happier if our mothers had not left us with another woman? That they should have been bringing us up themselves? Is that what you mean? When my parents were young my mother helped my father in our restaurant, and after me she had three more children. I know that my Aunt Marie – she was not married then – used to look after us as well. I always thought I had two mothers. That is better than one mother. I was always happy. Am I right to think like that?'

It was clear to Harold that his anti-feminist comments were being challenged and that he had to think quickly if he were to defend an attitude for which most women and some men would attack him. 'I'm sure you're right. But you were a special case. Your mother was there all the time, although her sister obviously helped her look after you. She probably helped her in the kitchen as well. You were part of a happy team from the moment you were born. That's probably why you like the group and why the group likes you. It's because you are a team player. But, for most people, whoever was responsible for bringing us up would have influenced how we turned out. The question is whether a child's birth mother is likely to make a better job of it than a paid helper rather than whether women should be treated as men in the workplace.'

They all agreed that logically the mother would be a better option but that this would mean denying women their right to a career.

'It was different for Luc,' said Harold. 'Aunt Marie obviously was a great help, but his mother was there all the time. She was only a stone's throw from the action. She was either in the kitchen helping his father with the cooking or upstairs making the beds.' He wondered why he didn't want women to have the same rights as men. He liked them as they were. Men as men were fine, too. But he didn't want women to be like men. It hadn't occurred to him before, but he was pleased that the group was entirely male. He didn't want women in the workplace. He wanted them at home, preferably in the kitchen and looking after him. 'I'm not an anti-feminist. I do like women. It's men I don't like very much.' The others looked at him curiously, no one being quite sure what he meant. He thought he should try to explain. 'Some men can be rough and very pushy. I don't like that. I don't even like it in women.' He thought for another moment or two. 'What I think I am is an anti-masculinist.'

The men said goodbye to one another and wandered off, pleased that they had coined a neologism. Harold was rather less pleased because he wasn't altogether sure what it was that he had actually meant.

FOUR

やや

'It was like I'd been running in a marathon,' Alex was saying to her friend Lola as they were leaving the gym. 'I was exhausted, I couldn't breathe. I didn't think I'd make it.'

Both of them knew that it was not likely to have been the exercise class that was responsible. She had thought she was coming down with something that morning and had spent most of the time sitting on an exercise bicycle chatting to one of the trainers to whom she had taken a fancy. This was hardly likely to bring her out into a sweat, although her heart might have been racing for reasons that had nothing to do with exercise. Lola thought that Alex's belief that the race went to the swift and that she must always run faster than anyone else to keep up might have had rather more to do with it.

Alex knew very well why she felt the way she did. She had been reminded that morning of something from her past that had continued to frighten her. It wasn't the first time she had thought that a catastrophe was about to happen. She wasn't sure what it was that had panicked her this time, although she suspected – as she had done many times before – that it had something to do with the death of her mother and older brother in a car accident when she was twelve. How she felt about that never entirely left her. Would she ever get over it? She'd had similar panic feelings immediately after the accident, and her GP had diagnosed post-traumatic stress. The stress had lasted for a good two years, but she had had therapy on and off for much longer because she had also been depressed. But how she had felt that morning was different. She was so terrified that she wondered whether she was going to collapse and die. It had to be more than just a panic attack; it was a feeling of losing out, of helplessness, of a belief that others would know by looking at her what was going on in her mind. She still had a heavy feeling in her chest. It had been too overwhelming and devastating for her to want to discuss it with anyone, even with Lola who was her best friend. Just thinking about it frightened her. She was terrified that the symptoms might come back.

She wanted Lola to know what had happened but not why she felt as she did. Talking about it made her feel worse. She tried to reassure herself that fear of the unknown was always more frightening than things that are familiar. That must be it, she told herself. It was because she didn't know why she was so terrified that morning, but somewhere in the back of her mind she thought she probably did.

Lola had even less of an idea of what Alex was going through. She thought of her friend as being oversensitive and someone who had had problems while growing up. She knew about her mother and brother being killed but not the details, since Alex rarely spoke of it. Lola thought Alex's father had been difficult to get on with after the accident, but her friend had never said much about him either. What she did know was that winning meant a lot to her. Whether the two were connected she had no idea. Alex was preoccupied with ambition and with wanting to get there – wherever 'there' was – before anyone else. She had felt that way since school. Playing games or passing examinations, as well as being excessively competitive or doing almost anything as long as it led to praise, had always been her priority. When she succeeded she felt better and her anxieties lessened, at least for a while.

Lola had never been sure of the nature of Alex's anxieties,

other than those connected with her mother's death, but she knew that she would be miserable for days if she thought that someone didn't like her. She had told Lola once that she would fantasize about being rescued from a commitment that was stifling her. What the commitment was Lola didn't know, but she felt it must be something that had happened to her years earlier as a child. Alex didn't know what it was either, but she thought of it as like claustrophobia, like being trapped, like being in a place from which she couldn't escape. What she didn't realize, because her feelings had become so habitual, was that it was depression and loss that trapped her and that praise, approval and acceptance not only acted as antidepressants but that she had become addicted to them.

Alex seldom allowed herself to think about her mother's death. She had never discussed it with any of her other school friends. She had only told Lola to whom she was particularly close. But the panic feelings that she was describing reminded her of the day more than fourteen years earlier when her father had explained that her mother and brother had been killed on their way home from the weekly shop. She had never forgotten what he had said. His words were as fresh in her mind as if he had spoken them just a few minutes earlier.

The head teacher had come into the classroom and told her that she had to go the nearby hospital where her father would meet her. He would be in reception. There had been an accident. That was all she said. Alex remembered that day vividly. It was exactly a week after her twelfth birthday. It was late afternoon, and French had just started. It didn't occur to her to ask for more information. At that age you do what you are told. The head teacher had asked whether she would like her to accompany her. Alex had said the hospital was only a few minutes away and she could manage by herself. She passed it every morning on her way to school.

She had run to school that morning from the farm where she lived with her parents and older brother because it was such a sunny day. Exuberant as always, she ran to the hospital not because she was anticipating disaster but because she wanted to tell her mother something. As she rushed up the steps into reception her father was standing by the front desk. He put his arms around her. Why is he doing this? she had asked herself. He hardly ever hugs me. Why isn't he at work? He's always at work in the afternoon. She was frightened and stared at him. She didn't recognize him. He seemed older and was shaking. She, too, began to shake. She remembered feeling very cold.

'What's wrong? Where's Mama?'

'Alex, something has happened. I want you to be strong.'

How could he have asked a twelve-year-old child to be strong? But what could else could he have said? Telling her that she could rely on his strength to see both of them through it might have been better. She had wanted to write his script even then.

She knew now that he didn't feel strong. He didn't even feel strong enough to pretend he was strong. He had no idea what to say to her. No idea how to address their situation. It was far outside his experience. It was the sort of thing her mother would have handled so much better. He should never have considered dealing with it himself. She sighed at the irony of it all.

She understood her father now far better than she had done as a child. She understood his anger, the sense of 'Why has she left this for me to deal with?' She thought she understood his thought processes at the time. He was probably trying to reassure himself that it was normal to think like that. He had known it was not normal. She knew even in those early moments that he had tried to think of the best way to put into words something he was fighting not to blank out. He would have wished to blank it out.

How could he tell his daughter that she no longer had a mother or an older brother?

'What is it, Papa? Tell me what it is!' She had wished he would hurry up because her anxiety was becoming unbearable.

'Mama was driving home from the shops with Andrew.'

He paused, and for a moment she recalled feeling that he was hurting her deliberately. It was a mental hurt, but it felt like a physical pain. She felt it in her whole body. He was prolonging her agony. He was punishing her by keeping her waiting. She had been convinced it had been deliberate. That's what men are like, she told herself. It was years before she could consider an alternative interpretation. Maybe he was too choked up to speak, too distressed to visualize and describe an event that he could not bear to think about, never mind describe to the child who was all that remained of his family.

'They turned off the motorway. They were almost home. Another car – it wasn't going fast – was coming towards them. A tyre blew out. The driver lost control. It wasn't his fault. They collided head on. There was a baby on the front seat of the other car. An ambulance came. They couldn't save any of them.' It seemed like an age to Alex before he said so quietly that she could scarcely hear him, 'They were all dead. All of them, in both cars, were dead.'

It was a long time ago, but she had never forgotten it. She would never forget it. It was the shock of it. Even now not a day passed when something – being a passenger in a car in a country lane, watching out for anything that could lead to an accident, bad driving, reading about accidents, seeing a road traffic accident on the television, hearing screaming tyres, ambulance sirens, being startled by a loud noise – would remind her of it. Why would she forget it? She often asked herself that question, but she knew remembering it kept her pain alive. She didn't want to forget it.

She wanted the pain. Through suffering, the guilt about what she often felt, not about her mother but about her brother, might one day be expiated.

Alex wanted to explain to Lola what had brought everything flooding back this time. But Lola didn't feel like being a shoulder for Alex right then. She had other things on her mind. She wanted to do some shopping. She had left her list at home and had forgotten what was on it, and she was trying to rewrite it in her head. Alex was definitely not on it. She was tired after the work-out. It was hot, and anyway she believed she had already heard most of what Alex wanted to say. She wasn't up to listening to it again. She decided that she would sort out her own problems first and then she could put her mind to Alex's.

But her friend was hard to ignore. She sighed imperceptibly, and she did listen. She thought of it more as a show of concern, more as a duty to someone who was closer to her than even her mother had been. But she didn't want to be an agony aunt. She was not qualified to help with anyone's emotional problems, particularly Alex's, who seemed to have far more than anyone else. Just hearing about them gave her a headache.

What about my problems? she asked herself. Who listens to how I feel? Alex never does. But such thoughts made her unhappy. She didn't want to feel that anyone close to her might not be interested in her. She knew she was like her friend in that respect. Anyway she seldom talked about herself, so she could hardly blame Alex for not listening. She sighed inwardly once more, composed her features into an expression which she hoped Alex would interpret as interest and then felt it safe to tune out much of what she was saying and concentrate on trying to recall what was on her list. Alex neither noticed nor cared. She had to talk about it. All she needed of her friend was that she was there. Both of them were tired, and neither of them was happy. Alex suddenly stopped talking. She had changed her mind. She felt too miserable to express her feelings. Not now. There would be time later.

The two young women had decided to take a year off. They called it a sabbatical. They had discovered that they were both virtually unemployable. They may have had good degrees from a good university, but they soon found out that much of the work available for theology graduates – as with other arts degrees – was in the field of education. They had tried teaching for about six years and didn't enjoy it. They had some savings and had paid off their student loans and were not too worried about money, but their careers were going nowhere. That was what parents and teachers had expected of them had failed to materialize. Their self-esteem, once reasonably high, was beginning to dissipate, and they could take only limited comfort from sharing how they felt with one another. Disappointments discussed were comforting but only to a point. So far there was no solution in sight. Forward planning, for the time being, consisted of no more than exercising regularly to be fit for the travels they had planned and a firm resolution to making more of an effort to work out what to do next.

Alex wondered whether she should have another try at entering the theatre world. The stage had always attracted her; whether for the right reasons or not she couldn't be sure. She had been to drama school for a year before deciding on the more certain world of teaching. None of her drama teachers had much encouragement to offer about her acting ability. When one of them told her, rather brutally, that she did not have a stage presence, confirming what she already suspected but which she hitherto had been reluctant to accept, she had called it a day. Thinking back over the past few years, she knew what she had liked then and liked now was admiration. Even picturing an audience, a

39

curtain call and applause made her feel good. It was something that might not do her any harm, but she was pleased to realize that there was no evidence that it would do her any good.

Franco in his café was not the only one whose attention had been drawn to the posse of men from the gym. What had puzzled the young women was that, although they all worked out together and were on first-name terms with everybody, they knew that they didn't quite fit in. They may have been *of* the men's group but they were not actually *in* their group. They thought it was because they were too young, but they soon discovered the real reason was that the men were more comfortable with other men. If anyone had accused them of sexism they would have denied it, but on the occasions when the girls sat with them in the canteen or chatted with them while working on one of the exercise machines they appeared slightly ill at ease. The girls felt as if they had intruded into a private conversation that had to be put on hold until later. They pretended neither to notice nor mind that they were left to make do with the conventional greetings when they turned up, the 'Let me get the coffee' routine afterwards and the polite 'See you next week' goodbyes when they left. They convinced themselves that they preferred separate tables and their own company. But there was something about the men – perhaps their camaraderie – to which they were attracted but from which they couldn't help but feel excluded.

FIVE

꿎

It was in a Chinese restaurant a week later that the men's group, most unusually, ran out of things to say to one another. It was a place they had been to before and which they all liked. Merlin Corcoran, a one-time actor known as Corker, who had spent most of his working life on tour playing minor Shakespearian roles, said it felt as if they were waiting for the director to show up rather than it being Harold's birthday. Corker only rarely came to the gym, but he was valued as a group member mainly, but not exclusively, because he impressed all of them by speaking almost entirely in quotes – usually from *Macbeth*. Corker accepted that most, if not all of them, were clichés but thought that anyone writing today would be very pleased to think that their words might still be in common use 400 years later.

Jerry was thinking of another Harold and another birthday party and hoped, almost certainly mischievously, that their lunch might run a similarly fractured course. But their Harold was not a playwright, and his concern for the next generation's intellect didn't run to the planning of meals. Harold liked them seeing him playing a role they wouldn't question. He was good at being someone he was not. He should have gone to drama school, but the stage was unknown territory in his family. He was certainly not ready to disclose who he was. Perhaps *what* he was might be more accurate. He knew it was customary for the birthday boy not only to pay for lunch but to order it, but since he invariably

41

claimed to have left such things to his wife he was able to convince everyone that he was incapable of untangling anything as simple as a menu. He pretended to be pleased when Luc took over. He wasn't really pleased, because he was neither an absent-minded academic nor did he think of himself as a fraud. He genuinely believed that he was something with whom others might have difficulty in coping. He would like to tell them about it. He would one day. He wasn't ready yet. In the meantime he would rely on Luc's expertise.

Luc loved cooking and food. He was in his element in restaurants and pubs and immediately stepped into the breach. He suggested that Harold tell the waiter, who was patiently stand-ing by the table while passing the time trying to light a candle – despite it being lunchtime not dinner and too draughty – to bring six fixed-price menus for the seven of them.

'Out, out, brief candle,' said Corker in a voice trained to be heard by everyone wherever he happened to be at the time. It was clearly a restaurant, but he was oblivious of the location. As usual, his only concern was that he be heard clearly. He had discovered long ago that the painfully whispered words uttered in his early life were not caused by a speech defect but by his belief that no one ever listened to anything he had to say. He eventually gave up. The struggle to be heard was too much. Even after he had found out that his mother could not hear him – it was before the days of antibiotics and a common problem – it took years of therapy to overcome his conviction that what he had to say was of no interest to anyone. The stage had helped him speak – but only when using other people's words. He still believed that his own would fall on deaf ears. He was certainly not addressing the Chinese waiter who had already left to tell the cook to put six lunches in the microwave.

As usual, they were sitting at a round table. It was their

preferred seating arrangement. It made them feel more of a piece, and a long table left the hard-of-hearing ones at the end too far out of the loop. Jerry had volunteered to telephone and book a round table in a quiet corner of the room. 'We've all got Aids,' he had explained to the waiter. 'Hearing aids,' he added after a pause. The Chinese waiter didn't laugh, but according to Jerry he was relieved when he had carefully deconstructed his request and explained that it was a joke. It was Jerry's turn to feel worried when the waiter said the chef liked a joke and he was going straight into the kitchen to translate it into Cantonese for him.

Although there were usually six or seven of them plus or minus one or two to allow for normal comings and goings, one chair remained empty. Silas the sculptor had failed to show up. He had not told anyone he would be absent, but no one commented on it. To come and go without explanation was a feature of the group's relationship with one another. They exercised their right to do as they liked, providing no one was put out by it. Not having to give reasons was a precious freedom, and they valued it highly. There were other freedoms which they had as yet not recognized. They were not trapped in an environment where either no one listened because they could not hear or where they were left alone with sorrows that could be addressed only by a concerned other.

Their mildly bizarre views had, over time, impressed upon them not racism, ageism or social niceties but a light-hearted chauvinism. In these social events, away from their interactions among the bicycles, treadmills and cross-trainers where they took life much more seriously than they did elsewhere, they would usually let their hair down and regress to a time that, if they thought about it at all, had long since passed for all of them and in one or two cases had possibly never been. None of them had wondered why in letting-their-hair-down mode they preferred to exclude women. If asked, they would have protested that women played a big role in their lives. They liked women. They had all had female lovers, most had been or still were married, and none claimed to be gay. Yet during their communal time-out they believed they could speak more freely in the absence of women. It would be some time before they realized that the only woman with whom they had all had problems was their mother and what they had to say was in one way or another a consequence of their upbringing and would almost certainly offend an updated version of her.

Although they had never explored why they found the presence of women faintly disagreeable, a discussion that never failed to fascinate all of them was marriage and its discontents. It was a subject that had been written about by one, sculpted about by another, misrepresented probably by all, put up with by most and ignored completely by Corker, who spoke only in his onstage voice about outings with his sacred (presumably celibate) aunt and who was thought by one or two of them to be homosexual. But today even that topic remained closed.

On an oft-recalled occasion a member of the group who had given up coming to the gym and who clearly hadn't been in the group long enough to become attuned to its unwritten rules – or what one disgruntled partner had described as its prejudices – had brought his wife Angelica to their luncheon club. She came just once. Everyone was polite, but the general consensus had been that her presence had upset the fine balance of their non-representational, cross-generational, gender-specific conversation. She had been rather admired for being sufficiently sensitive to recognize this, but that was as far as it went. There had been no bonding. Their favourite abstraction, leaving aside their views about women, was not about the day-to-day uniformities from which they had temporarily escaped but about the esoteric vagaries that made up their prejudices.

For a while no one spoke, and the silence was becoming oppressive. Luc, usually very talkative and much appreciated for his concern for others nurtured by a lifetime of caring for the gastronomic needs of city workers, thought he would start the ball rolling by bringing up the famous Angelica's one-off appearance. 'At least Eddie's partner gave us something to talk about. We've been lunching out on that one for a long time.'

There was no response. There was very little left to say about Angelica whose mother might have thought of her as a little angel but who hadn't come across as anything like one to any member of the group other than perhaps her partner.

Neither did Corker's possibly inappropriate reassurance that 'Stones have been known to move and trees to speak' have much effect on a rare lassitude that affected them all. Apart from a few almost inaudible mutters, and Jerry's brief reflection on why Luc had said 'lunching' instead of the more usual but definitely in this context less correct 'dining', the group remained lost in thought. Jerry, who hadn't worked out that morning because he had sprained his shoulder ('picked up a shoulder injury', as he put it to show the others he was *au fait* with current sports terminology) and who had come especially for Harold's birthday lunch, felt that he was playing a part in a Mike Leigh film. Who would hand around the script, pose the questions, tease out the answers, conduct a metaphorical choir and squeeze a sound or two from a deflated bagpipe? They sat almost in silence, waiting.

None of them seemed comfortable with the silence. Did they feel it as threatening, an empty space, of nothingness, an unwanted disconnect from the world that enclosed them? Did it remind them of loneliness, of solitary confinement, of no one being there – feelings familiar to those who as infants may have been left too long with no one but themselves to comfort them? It was Drago who quietly commented that lonely gratification was only acceptable when shared with someone. But they were all in too sombre a mood to smile at Drago's minor witticism or, more likely, his problem with the language.

Jerry wondered whether Corker was right. Maybe they were like infants waiting to be given a script, not by a non-existent mother but by the director. But there was no director, because no one trusted directors. They had all been let down by a director of one sort or another, whether maternal or paternal. Directors, for all of them, were long in their pasts. They sometimes felt that they were a group of the forsaken, there only for one another. They liked to believe that they needed no one else. Even if there happened to be an alpha male on the day he could be relied on only for a limited time, and alpha females, in whom no one had much belief or confidence, had anyway ruled themselves out by their gender. It was either the most elated or the most troubled who would slip effortlessly into a 'listen to me' role. The rest went along with whoever happened to be on the crest of his wave at the time, especially if he had already proved his worth by offering remedies to those in their troughs. No one wanted to play that role or any other role today.

They usually looked forward to their birthday lunches. Regressing to carefree irresponsibility for two or three hours and a freedom of speech, by the content of which no one was ever offended, was an experience to which they felt they could happily become addicted. It was not to be missed. One or two on diets might occasionally pay lip service, or more likely mouth service, to not eating too much and rely on conversation to satisfy oral needs. But today no one was speaking. There was something different in the air, a subtle change, a foreboding, a chill, a cloud. Something was up. Could it be to do with the journey Benedict had suggested they were on or something else that they had intuitively taken a collective view about?

Jerry's thoughts went to those they referred to simply as 'the other group' – one diametrically different from theirs. By comparing and contrasting the other group's interests with their own might at least give him something else to think about and possibly talk about. The others were mixed gender, never went to a restaurant for lunch, preferred a sandwich and a cup of tea in a pub before going home and behaved as if they were oldies performing in an episode of *Last of the Summer Wine*. Their conversation was not noted for laugh-a-minute esoteric undertones as theirs was. They spoke only in Realpolitik. They had bonded but loosely, very unlike the bonding that Jerry and the others experienced. Discussions about the bus service (other than Drago's allegorical one) or those gym members who had been absent recently were seldom of interest to their group.

A prominent member of the other group had been Billy. On the rare occasions when his name was mentioned it was hardly ever with affection. He was a unifying factor because no one liked him, and he was referred to by everybody (although not to his face, since it was thought that he could be violent) as Billy the Baker because he had once claimed – untruthfully – to be a retired master baker. It turned out, according to a neighbour, that he was a plumber. Upgrading his status was generally thought to be an attempt to impress Caroline, an attractive 55-year-old raven-haired ex-pole dancer with whom he had fallen madly but unrequitedly in love.

Billy was not lovable. He was aggressive and occasionally threatening, particularly when any other male addressed a few words to his fantasy girlfriend. He had recently persuaded her to try out a new exercise machine in a small secluded area of the gym adjoining the dance studio. Leaning over her while offering unasked-for instruction he contrived to make it look, possibly not deliberately, as if he was simulating an intimacy, mechanical in fact but sexual in appearance, that was embarrassing to her and to everyone else.

Billy's most recent claim to fame was of falling off the roof of his home. Fallen, jumped or pushed. Someone may have known, but very few cared. Jerry wondered why no one was talking about it since his sudden death had been reported in the local newspaper. It was easily the most exceptional event that had happened at the gym since a gay member in the changing-room forgot where he was and got carried away by male bodies. Most of the others had not known where to look.

Jerry, who was, as usual, convinced that more was going on than met the eye, thought he knew why Billy's sudden death was going unremarked. He didn't suspect anyone of actually murdering him, although as he looked around the table possibly one or other of them might, at some time, have wanted to. That might be a good reason, he thought, for not talking about him – or at least not drawing unwanted attention to wishful thinking that was better kept to himself.

The silence, now oppressive, was broken by the arrival of the food and the polite 'After yous' they felt obliged to utter while it was handed around. The drinks had also arrived, and a silent collective sigh of relief began to overwhelm everyone. Tongues unlocked, and conversation, food-related at first, changed into an overwhelming outflow of suppressed feeling.

Benedict, usually very articulate but now so breathless with emotion that he was having difficulty in getting his words out, spoke into what remained of the silence. 'I've got a friend with a problem. He's fallen madly in love with an absolutely amazing woman. He met her by chance while they were on a rock-climbing holiday in Scotland. She was on her own, and so was he. They have an enormous emotional understanding. He's never experienced anything like it. He had huge problems with his present girlfriend, and they've been on the verge of calling it a day for a long time. In fact, they have more or less done it. But what he doesn't understand is why he can't bring himself to tell her about his new girlfriend, finalize the break and then move in with her.'

Benedict did know why he could not tell his former live-in partner about his new girlfriend. Always self-conscious and needing desperately to be liked even by someone with whom he had fallen out, and anyway hating to be thought of as fickle, he was convinced that he would be unable to tolerate his former girlfriend's disapproval when she came to discover that he had got over her so quickly. He looked around the table to check his companions were listening. They were. They were not only listening but talking. All of them at the same time – but not about the predicament of Benedict's supposed friend for whom he might have obtained some helpful advice but about problems, some of them similar, experienced at some time or another by every one of them.

What was puzzling to all of them, but particularly to Jerry, was why Benedict's predicament had triggered such an overwhelming response in everyone. Soon the table was so awash with the sudden change from general to personal that to Benedict, always whimsical – at least when he wasn't spending time worrying about whether people liked him – it seemed that soon there would hardly be any room on the table for the food. Had their unexpected outpourings something to do with the round table, which perhaps had drawn them together into a single entity, an all-boys group of musketeers whose thoughts and feelings coalesced? Were all of them not so much being confessed to as being given an opportunity to express their own pent-up problems?

Perhaps the empty chair contributed in some way to what was going on? They had all commented on it as they sat down. Had they recognized some significance in it which they could not explain? Was it possible or, more likely, fanciful that they felt it as an empty throne, a reminder of the presence, albeit invisible, of a father, holy or otherwise? Could they be looking for a parent whose approval they had seldom experienced?

What Jerry ultimately thought, in what he considered to be a flash of insight, was that the reason why no one wanted to speak when they first sat down for lunch was because of the death of Billy. Not because any of them had anything to do with it – he had probably not been murdered anyway – but because they may have sensed the presence of a judgemental presence sitting in the empty chair, which no one seemed keen to confront. They would, of course, have had to have done something wrong. Not as the murderous Macbeth had perhaps – but they could all be blamed for something. Even the most law-abiding experienced mild anxiety while being regarded by security cameras in a supermarket. No one felt entirely beyond reproach, not even those who were. Who was the reproachful ghost at their feast? It felt like a Banquo.

Was the pilgrimage that Benedict had spoken of a journey that would end not in death but in a life redeemed because of the all-forgiving presence of 'our father in heaven' in the empty chair? Was it insight into what they had in common that had drawn them together as well as a desire for physical fitness? Were they all offenders of one sort or another, or was it something else of which they were as yet unaware that was acting as a magnet? Something or someone had to be sitting at the table with them. Whatever or whoever it was seemed to all of them, for a moment, to unite them.

'Where does the truth lie?' asked Jerry.

Corker's quote to the effect that one should be true at least to oneself should have wrapped it up. But Benedict's far-away look stayed with most of them.

The others remained listening only to their own unspoken thoughts.

SIX

❧

If today was different for the group of men it was certainly different for Alex and Lola. They were on their way to a matinée. *King Lear* had been a favourite of Alex's late mother. Lola thought that it would almost certainly encourage Alex to talk about her, but to her relief she seemed to have put aside her memories of the accident and instead chose to talk about the men they exercised with.

'I wonder why they never ask us to have lunch with them.' Alex was genuinely puzzled but tried not to sound disappointed.

'I don't think I'd go even if they were to.'

They both knew this to be untrue, because they wished the men would show at least some interest in them. It was obvious that a strong rapport existed among the males. The two young women would occasionally overhear an exchange of repartee that made everyone laugh and in which they would have liked to have been included. But there was more to it than that. They were not exactly sure what it was, but there was something about them to which they felt drawn. Alex told Lola that she thought it was because she didn't like to be left out of anything. It was the opposite of Groucho Marx's self-deprecating comment that any club that wanted him as a member wouldn't be one he would care to join. Alex wanted to be in their club precisely because she had not been invited to join it. Knowing Alex as she did, Lola couldn't help but agree with her. Feeling they had been turned away induced a familiar sense of gloom in the two of them. They scarcely knew them, and yet being ignored was distressingly familiar. They knew nothing of what the men talked about or of their closeness to one another, but were Alex and Lola asked they would have admitted to experiencing a similar closeness not just to each other but, surprisingly, to the men.

'They're actually very nice,' Alex remarked and wondered why she had said this when she knew nothing whatever about them. She knew only that she needed them to be very nice for reasons she was not clear about.

She had slipped into a reflective mood, into a silent debate that required no external participation and which added to Lola's feelings of exclusion. She had never become used to her friend's idiosyncratically intermittent style of communication. She hated it when she stopped talking to her. She wouldn't have minded if she spoke to the people who lived inside her head when she was on her own, but she didn't like her doing it when she was with her. Hours would pass when Lola and probably the rest of the world ceased to exist for Alex. Lola occasionally challenged her friend and asked her what she was thinking about. She had long since decided against asking her with whom she was in conversation. She had tried it just once only to be met with a stare of total incomprehension.

Alex was still wondering why she had said that the men were very nice. Was it because they behaved as if she didn't exist? She knew she hated that. Or was it because she was surprised that men could be very nice? Maybe she was hoping that one of them, or perhaps all of them, might think she was nice. But which one of them might that be? And anyway did it matter? They were all tarred with the same brush.

What did that mean? Did she really believe that all men behaved badly? It was an absurd generalization, but something about it rang true. She thought fleetingly of her father. She tried to remember what it was, but despite returning to it from time to time she couldn't throw any further light on it. She was on more familiar ground when she asked herself with what brush she would like to be tarred.

Could it be beauty? She would be pleased with that. She accepted in her happier moments that she was attractive. People had told her so. She had a healthy look about her, probably from the gym, but she still needed to double-check in mirrors and shop windows. She knew there were some women who couldn't leave their home before spending hours preparing their face for exposure to the world. Was how they looked more important to them than how they behaved? She wasn't like that. But her blonde hair, usually tied in a ponytail, had to look absolutely right, and she was pleased when her blue eyes occasioned more than an fleeting glance by passers-by. She was tall and slim, but, despite that, no one in the men's group reacted towards her in the way she thought most men not only would but should.

Luigi, the owner of the sandwich bar she and Lola patronized, was completely different. His welcome was over-the-top, flirtatious even. She knew his manner was induced by commercial rather than emotional feelings and meant nothing more than his belief that his customers expected something typically Italian of him, but the men at the gym could behave like he did if they wanted to play games. That they showed no interest whatsoever in flirting with her or Lola distressed and disappointed her.

They began a slow drift towards their bus-stop almost half-way into an area famous for its fashion stores. It was a shopper's paradise; probably attracting more lookers than buyers. But neither of them was interested in shoes or dresses right then. Window-shopping could wait another day. Alex decided that she just wanted to talk, and her friend, who had not wanted to listen, prepared herself for the inevitable.

Lola switched off the familiar resentment that she usually experienced when Alex carried on with whatever she was doing as if she wasn't with her and began concentrating again on what she was actually saying. Talking clearly at first and then in a hard-to-comprehend mumble, Alex embarked on a distorted monologue, a verbal jigsaw that she expected Lola to piece together. Her story was not easy to interpret, because not only did she seem to be experiencing flashbacks but many apparently irrelevant and fleeting thoughts interspersed in the jerky ebb and flow disrupted its narrative thread. Much of it was familiar to Lola. She had not heard all of it before, but she had heard enough of it to be able to pick up on where Alex had got to.

She knew what had troubled her friend ever since their relationship had evolved into the feeling of oneness found usually in sisters. They were both just over twelve on the day Alex had been chosen by her drama teacher to play Juliet in the school play. It was a day that had started out joyously. Alex had no idea how calamitous it was to become later that afternoon. She had told her friend that she was running to the hospital because she had been summoned there by her father. But at the same time she was running to tell her mother about her part in the play. Lola had never been able to understand why it had not occurred to Alex to wonder why she had been summoned to meet her father at the hospital. They were adults before Lola discovered that Alex's confusion might have been partly the result of a head injury from a fall on the hospital's steps.

Alex was always running. Running towards or running away or running to keep her weight down or simply running to impress. It seemed obvious on this occasion that she thought she was running to hear her mother tell her how clever she was to have been given a leading role in a play. She clearly had no idea that she was running to meet her father who was preparing to tell her that her mother and brother had been killed in a traffic accident. But the running continued even after her mother's death. Sooner or later it would have to stop.

For a moment Lola had a prophetic image of Alex running to meet her Romeo. She had, after all, been going to play Juliet all those years ago. She dismissed the thought as being disappointingly fanciful. She wondered when she could expect her own Romeo to turn up. So far there had been no one even remotely interested in her. She pushed the thought away, not because it didn't interest her, because it did, but she reminded herself that she was supposed to be listening to Alex's story, not ruminating about her romantic needs.

Lola returned to safer ground and wondered why Alex thought anyone would have been sufficiently interested in school Shakespeare to tell her mother about her daughter's role before Alex had done so herself. It was hardly a world-shattering event. As it happened, it had turned out to be an event the consequences of which had affected Alex ever since.

Lola could have asked her why being first with the news was so important to her friend. But she had never done that because she imagined that Alex probably didn't know. She would have told her if she had known. Maybe even after all this time it was still too painful to discuss. It didn't occur to Lola that her friend might have wanted to have been the first with the news. Not in any kind of contest but to have been the first born, the preferred child. The role that had been played by her brother.

Lola tried instead to imagine the girls in Alex's class walking home. They would probably be giggling and talking about boys. None of them would be hurrying. No one would want to be first in anything. She thought about Romeo again. She wondered why looking for one till now had never been more than a passing thought. Did she really want one? And if she didn't want one, why not? She asked herself this question hesitantly. She wondered as she had sometimes wondered before whether it was because men were not her type. Might she prefer women? She was only slightly shocked. She knew that she did like women, and she had occasionally fantasized about sex with a woman. She reassured herself that she need not be too concerned because she knew she was aroused by men and that should she want to be a mother her sexual preferences wouldn't be a problem.

She would have liked to have gone on musing in this vein, but her thoughts were interrupted by Alex making it clear that there were several more items on her agenda that she expected Lola to address. She didn't put it like that, but Lola knew that other people's problems were never particularly high on the list of things that interested her. She prepared herself for Alex returning to talking about the men at the gym. But, instead, she switched to something else.

'Why wasn't I like my friends? Why did I always have to be a winner, always first at things? Exams, sport, buying the new *Harry Potter*, being a star?' Alex didn't wait for an answer. She knew that being a loser was not for her. Being born a loser was enough to be going on with. 'I wish I understood myself better. I wish I wasn't so unhappy a lot of the time.'

She gave Lola a questioning look as if to ask whether she was withholding important information that would magically put things right were she to share it but said nothing. Lola's return look, resigned but impatient, hinted: why is it taking so long for you to grow up? They both knew that some parents fussed over their first child more than they did with their second. Maybe Alex's craving for approval had something to do with that. Would they have loved her more if she had been a boy or the eldest child? Alex would have liked that to have been the reason, the only reason, but she knew, with hindsight, that it might have been the case when she was very young, but more recent events had put a different gloss on it.

She realized that her thoughts were in danger of becoming circular. She would have to stop before she spent any more time locked into tail-chasing daydreams. Ironically, being the younger of two children might once have been a problem, but now being an only child was the problem. Losing her mother was one thing. She would never get over it. But it wasn't her fault. Her brother's death was something else. She still felt guilty about it. She had wished it upon him. She had often wished he had never been born. She tried to convince herself that wishing someone had not been born was not the same as wishing them dead, but the cold cruelty of her thought about her mother's involvement for the deaths of four people, including herself, made that difficult.

It was not that she had hated Andrew; in fact she loved him despite his unacceptable curiosity about her developing femininity before he was killed. It was his status in the family she had hated. He had been number one, and more than fourteen years after his death he was still number one. She had been unable to let go of him and until she did so she could never win. Trying to be first would get her nowhere. She would be an also-ran for the rest of her life, a runner-up in a one-horse race. There were winners and losers. She was born a loser. She tried to reassure herself that she had genuinely loved Andrew, but the guilt that had made her feel that she could never have a life because her brother had not had one, stayed with her. Living to eighteen was not a life.

It struck her that wishing she had not had an older brother was hardly a crime. If it was, huge numbers of people must be guilty of it. She knew what it was. It had suddenly come to her. She was suffering from survivor's guilt. It was not 'why me? it was 'why not me?' There had been a documentary about the Holocaust on the television recently. It had explained why Holocaust survivors often felt guilty. It had given an example of two brothers, one of whom had survived because he was strong enough to be a slave labourer and the other murdered because he was too weak to work. She could understand guilt in that context. She understood for the first time that she didn't have to feel guilty. Andrew's death wasn't her fault. She could not blame herself for it. It was becoming clearer. He had not gone to his death in her place. She could never have gone shopping with her mother that day. It was a school day. She was not even at home.

She stopped thinking in flashbacks, but she knew there was still a lot of thinking to do before she could abandon her sense of guilt, her need to punish herself and, above all, her inability to let go of her brother and move on. Lola, jolted out of the half-listening, half-preoccupied mode in which she often found herself when she was with her friend, waited for Alex's familiar although essentially confusing monologue to resume. But she didn't speak. She was thinking. Lola might not understand. She didn't really understand it herself. They were once a family of four. Now there were only two. All that had come of it was that she had got to know her father better. She didn't want to talk about it.

She could have a life, she thought, a life with Lola. There would be no Andrew, no father. No men. She might be safe from her attacking conscience. She didn't really like men. She wanted them to admire her, but she didn't like them. She thought what a world without men would be like. She smiled for the first time that day. It was a grim smile. Anyone seeing it would feel uneasy rather than be reassured by it. Lola took her hand and thoughtfully squeezed it; she had always been more insightful than her friend. Alex wondered whether Lola had known what

58

she was thinking or whether it was what she hoped she had been thinking.

Alex's thoughts drifted back to the gym. They had stayed for coffee that morning and been sitting in what Lola referred to as their purdah position, at the long table in the canteen and a few yards from the group. Three or four strangers were also sitting at it. Two were middle-aged men apparently with heart problems discussing whether exercise would really protect them from further attacks and another two were women whose conversation centred on their frequent visits to the doctor. They, too, were talking about postponing death, although rather less directly. They were discussing how difficult it was to cross the road not so much because of the heavy traffic but because the green man on the pedestrian crossing didn't remain illuminated long enough to allow slower older people to reach the other side in safety.

At the time Alex had scarcely registered this mundane conversation, but now she thought of it as confirming her belief that perhaps the race really did go to the swift. That, together with her memories of her mother's and her brother's gruesome end, made her realize for the first time that running, or at least crossing the road swiftly to avoid being killed, might have a purpose.

Getting on with it was not just a measure of scholastic or sporting skill but actually a life-saver. Might her conscience, as ever demanding retribution for her sinful thoughts, be mollified by the speed with which she was able to appease it or even escape from it? She was surprised by how confused her thinking was becoming and how devious she would have to be to avoid the punishment which for years she genuinely believed to be her due. She wondered briefly whether she had deliberately chosen *King Lear* that afternoon because children exposed to unreasonable expectations from demanding fathers were what she expected from life. Did she have that in mind when she was running to tell

59

her mother she would be playing a young woman in love? She didn't think so, nor did she want to think she was hurrying to tell her she would be playing an innocent child who some might consider had allowed herself to be seduced by Romeo. She might once have hoped that it might have been the former but was interested that she was now considering another option. She found both of them distasteful and quickly dismissed them from her thinking, but not before accepting that Juliet had not done much to resist the temptations of under-age sex. She derived some comfort from the thought that although Romeo and Juliet was a tragedy it did at least bring two squabbling families together. It might even have helped her cope with her problem with Andrew had it been on the curriculum at school instead of *A Midsummer Night's Dream*.

Despite her resolve to stop her depressive thinking she began to fast-forward events of the past with the images moving too swiftly to be identified. She would give it up after this one. One last time she told herself. Glancing only for a moment at Lola who had turned her head briefly to look in a shop window, Alex in a beat had returned to the events of the day fourteen years earlier when, pressing a mental playback button, she had a vivid image of what she did on her return from school on the day that her mother died.

She had pushed open the front door of their farmhouse, flung her books on to the hall chair and called out, 'It's me', and waited for the usual response that her tea was ready. Her confusion told her that there had been no sound from the kitchen that fateful day. Instead what she had heard terrified her. Her father was sobbing. The fact was that she knew that none of that had occurred and that she had known of her mother's death by her father telling her that day, but she could only cope with her version of events.

She knew, because she had been told, that she had fallen in

the hospital, that she had injured her head and that she had had a level of memory loss that a physician had later described as severe. She knew also that her recollection for some of the events of that day, although much improved, would remain distorted. The mental picture that she was describing to Lola was always the same. Her compulsion to play it again as if it had actually happened never left her.

As if she was watching a television replay of a documentary that she needed to study she noted that her memories of calling 'Mum, Mum, where are you?' were being overwhelmed by other louder more insistent sounds and more vivid memories. She saw herself running up the stairs to her parents' bedroom and slipping down the snake that waited for the one whose lucky number had not come up. She knew that it had been the stone steps leading out of the hospital reception area down which she had fallen, leading to the ward where her mother had been taken, but it was the stone floor of her home that she was describing to herself. Her head was throbbing. Light, vivid at first then fading, was leading her into darkness, into forgetfulness. Then she recalled standing up and walking slowly towards her mother wanting to tell her about her fall, seeing her mother in her mind's eye now as clearly as she must have seen her then, still and silent, covered only by a sheet. Her mother was icy to her touch. Why was she so cold? Had she pulled the blankets over her? She told herself that she had found out that her mother's coldness had been beyond simple remedies, but Alex knew that terrible things must have happened while she had been unconscious. She had been distracted by her father's voice saying, 'I've something to tell you.'

She knew that she had played and replayed that scene innumerable times since it had happened, but she was unable to stop herself from repeating it for her friend. Each time she did so it sounded different. She knew also that sometimes she would try to change the sequence of events – to move backwards to a time when the accident could have been avoided. A one-second pause in the ghastly drama was all she needed to change the course of history. A fleeting half-smile warmed her face as she thought what a second might have achieved in 1914. The Archduke's assassin would have missed his target. Over 35 million lives would have been saved. Previously her memory had taken her back only to her dead mother and her father's reactions on that day. She had never been able to think of anything else. She wondered whether she was getting over it at last.

She knew that one of the things that had kept the memory of it so vivid was her father's voice in the hospital reception, although she thought she had heard it at her home. She had been startled by his voice. It had not sounded like him. It was weaker, less authoritative.

She had asked him a question that she now knew came from her other memory. She had hoped it would bring normality to a situation that had become increasingly frightening. She knew the answer. 'Mama's so cold. Doesn't she need another blanket?'

'He didn't think much of that idea,' she told Lola in a voice that she hoped was becoming lighter but she knew remained grim.

He had held out his hands to her instead. 'Papa loves you, Alex. Papa will look after you.'

She had no doubt that he had said that. It wasn't a false memory. It was at that moment that she knew beyond any doubt that her mother was dead. Neither wishful thoughts nor the power of denial nor an appeal to higher authority could change what had happened. It was too late. She began to feel weepy and hoped that Lola wouldn't notice. But she did notice and, as sensitive as ever, put her arm around her shoulders. Alex was comforted, but her thoughts refused to leave that day; the worst day of her life. She recalled hoping that she had misheard her father. Hope had come and as quickly gone. A sense of detachment had distanced her from a situation with which she was too frightened to cope. She didn't want to be part of it. She had never wanted to be part of it. Nothing was real. Perhaps she was somewhere else. She remembered looking at her feet. But they were still attached to the floor. She had gone nowhere. A drama was taking place. A terrifying Grand Guignol. There was a part in it for her, but there would never be one for her mother. Was she dreaming? Would she wake up? Had she imagined it? She had been chosen for the school play because of her imagination. She would look in on her mother on the way. She would be there, sleeping late. She had been tired lately. But the sinking feeling in her chest and the weakness in her legs reminded her that what had happened was real. She was sure – or had she hoped? – that her father had wanted to say something to her. He had looked for words of comfort but could find none. He needed them for himself. He had none to spare for his daughter.

Alex told Lola how each morning when she awoke she would listen for the comforting sounds of the house: her mother's voice in the kitchen, the radio, the sound of the vacuum, the cleaning lady starting her day. But after the accident there was no sound, only silence. For a long time afterwards, mainly in the mornings, she explained to her friend that she had found breathing difficult because of the heaviness in her chest, in her head, in her mind. She would go outside into the fresh air, into the garden, anywhere. Time also confused her because of her head injury. On one occasion, it might have been months after the accident, she thought that only an hour had passed since she had left school that afternoon. She had been shocked when she discovered it was the following day. She had stared at the copse and the gate that kept the sheep from wandering, but she saw only sadness and regret. One day seemed clearer than the others. The sun was setting and the leaves were dying, the grass was browning and the swallows were leaving. She was cold. Was it the summer that was coming to an end – or was it her life?

She looked at her friend walking by her side. She may not have a mother, but she did have a friend. Was that enough? She wasn't sure. She thought again of the men's group. She was sure that one of them would be interested in how she felt. But Lola knew that, at least for a while, Alex's distorted memories of what until then had been an uneventful life had faded. Now back in the present they continued following another thread that was slowly untangling.

SEVEN

❦

Silas slowly puffed his way up the stairs into the canteen. He didn't see himself as a short overweight middle-aged, reasonably successful sculptor in need of a haircut and other forms of care that he wasn't getting, although everyone else seemed to. He knew only that as the absentee occupier of the empty chair at Harold's birthday party a week earlier he had stayed at home because he thought no one liked him. He had come to the gym that morning to test, not for the first time, whether that was actually the case.

He found two of the others talking excitedly about the various attempts that had been made over the years to date Shakespeare's sonnets. Benedict and Jerry were so involved in discussing Renaissance poetic themes that might shed some light on the order in which the 154 sonnets were written that neither of them looked up. Silas looked even more despondent than usual. When he rather pointedly moved Jerry's coat so that he could sit down they dragged themselves out of the late sixteenth century to greet him, an effort of which he was only too well aware and which he expected but none the less resented.

Benedict thought he knew how Silas felt. He stood up and with a vaguely conciliatory 'I'll get you some coffee' left Silas to talk to Jerry. Silas tried to feel companionable towards Jerry, but he seldom found himself in accordance with his slant on life. He had not told anyone this, because he thought it might introduce a discordant note for people who left home twice a week believing that they had found a peculiarly gratifying form of harmony in the gym. He usually included himself in this group, although unlike the others he occasionally had reservations about it. Anyway, he told himself, they needed his expertise, and maybe, for all he knew, they actually needed him. He knew he needed them most of the time. He cheered up slightly. What he thought he wanted from them was their energy, their vitality and their friendship. He knew it was on offer if he could bring himself to be less anxious about the possibility of it one day being withdrawn altogether or sometimes, as at that moment, when it seemed to be only marginally available.

Apart from being a sculptor of some note – Silas was especially skilled at creating bronzes of small children – he was knowledgeable about most things electronic. His friends at the gym were impressed with his ability to fix things. Whenever anyone had problems with computers, mobile phones or digital cameras Silas would know what to do. He thought of himself as obliging and helpful and found it hard to understand why he had begun to feel that, instead of being pleased that people valued him, he felt instead that he was being exploited.

Sometimes when he was able to think more clearly about himself he realized that he wasn't really happy to be good at the day-to-day things with which some would never be able to cope. He put it down to having been forced into a do-it-yourself lifestyle as a child because there had not been anyone else to do things for him. That wasn't something he wanted to be reminded of. That must be it, he told himself. They all assumed he was self-sufficient because he could do everything. He didn't want to do everything. He wanted people to do things for him for a change. They never had and even now seldom did. He knew that once he began to ruminate about his neglectful upbringing his mood would change and he would look around for someone to blame. It was never difficult to find a scapegoat. But he didn't want to do that just now. Despite his resolve not to take out his anger on someone he realized that he was thinking of doing just that. It wasn't Benedict's fault, but it felt like it.

Benedict was taking his time fetching the coffee. He wished he would hurry. He had been offered something; he knew it was only coffee, but he wasn't bringing it. It was promises, always promises. No one ever delivered. Nothing ever changed.

Being alone with Jerry was becoming increasingly uncomfortable. He didn't want to talk to Jerry because he resented being questioned, and Jerry didn't want to speak to Silas because he found his hypersensitivity irritating. Silas could spot, although he pretended not to be looking, that Benedict had given up his position in the café queue because he had begun to talk to Robert, a deaf Australian who exercised only sporadically. Because his visits to the gym were rare, his friends tended to resume discussions they had begun sometimes several months earlier. For Robert to bring Benedict up to date was obviously going to take a good deal of time and shouting. Silas could hear Benedict asking Robert what he thought about some national news. Benedict had obviously forgotten about the coffee and forgotten about Silas. He would either have to get it himself or stay and be civil to Jerry.

'What have you been up to lately? Haven't seen you for a while,' remarked Jerry

Silas was so annoyed by Benedict's absentmindedness, which he was doing his best to persuade himself wasn't deliberate, that his response was even more monosyllabic and curt than he had intended. It was so brief that he decided to repeat it, making it seem even more aggressive than it had been in the first place.

'Nothing. Nothing. Absolutely nothing. I've not been up to

anything.' He couldn't help himself. He was now becoming more than usually irritated with Jerry, who was not to blame for Benedict's forgetfulness, but it felt like it.

He reminded himself that what he didn't like about Jerry were his questions. He was always making enquiries or whatever policemen did. What did he mean, what have I been up to? Why does he want to know? It's not his business. I'm not a criminal. I wouldn't dream of trusting him with anything confidential. He would tell everyone. Silas was growing angrier. He was also aware that much of what he was feeling was because he had grown up to experience all authority – whether teachers, the police, father figures in general or traffic wardens, particularly traffic wardens, he thought – with resentment.

He felt slightly better when he reminded himself that it was hardly surprising that he felt as he did given his terrible childhood. He also remembered that his therapist had told him to think about what others might really mean when they asked him a question and that he should try to challenge his suspicions. Check them against reality, she had said. Silas had thought it a good idea at the time but had never actually done it. Perhaps he should give it a try. He began by asking himself what it could be that wasn't Jerry's business and what was it about him he could not trust. Anything would be better than the frustrating outcome of his usual discussions with him!

He decided that it must be the problem he was having with trying to give up internet dating. His interest in the internet and the various social-networking sites he was involved in was definitely not something he wanted Jerry to know about. He didn't want anyone to know about it. It was something of which he was not proud. Why did he do it? He didn't know. He just did it. Something drove him to it. It wasn't his fault. He was just looking for friends to chat with.

He knew that wasn't entirely true. It wasn't just chatting. He told himself that you couldn't have too many friends. But that wasn't quite his problem. Jerry knew nothing about him or about anything else that he had been up to lately and probably didn't want to, but Silas was reacting as if he was doing his best to find out. He began to see what his therapist meant and calmed down. Jerry was merely using a harmless opening gambit that had hit a raw nerve.

Anyway, internet dating was no different from going to the supermarket. Shopping for a companion was no different from shopping for breakfast cereal. He never bought food on the internet, even though it might be cheaper. He always liked to see what he was getting. Internet dating allowed him to look before buying and being able to return whatever it was if it wasn't fit for purpose. Was that all it meant to him? He liked to think it wasn't, but he knew that he invariably abused internet dating because he considered it a good way of satisfying his sexual needs. He disapproved of that in others. He was close to disapproving of it in himself, particularly since he was as guilty of misrepresentation as he assumed everyone else was. He invariably lied about his identity, his social status, his financial status and his appearance, even to the extent of posting pictures of much younger versions of himself on social networking sites.

Jerry looked up from his free newspaper and said, 'Been going out much?'

'No. Too busy on the internet, speed-dating.'

'Good idea. It's better than going to the pub and drinking on your own.'

Silas couldn't believe it. He was shocked. What had made him say that? It had just slipped out. He hoped Jerry thought he was joking.

Jerry, however, was bored. There was nothing interesting in

the newspapers, and there was no conversation he could get his teeth into with Silas. He was fed up with his companion's attempts at humour. He muttered an almost inaudible goodbye and left without even saying 'See you next week.' Silas now had no one to talk to and no one, other than himself, with whom to be angry. He felt even more rejected and miserable. Thinking about girls had probably brought it on. Or perhaps it was Jerry's fault. He needed someone to talk to who would understand him. He was sorry he had come to the gym. He should have stayed at home and carried on trying to network. Things had been bleak lately, but he must be due to get lucky sooner or later.

Benedict was still talking to the deaf Australian. He might return at any minute with or without the coffee, but he couldn't be relied on to be helpful. He was being forced to think rather than do. Silas began a familiar conversation with himself. It had never provided him with any answers. He knew only that it had to do with wanting to be with someone who cared about him, someone who would take an interest in him, someone who would befriend him. No one had ever done that. A woman might. He thought back to his brief relationship with Jilly who had abandoned him after four dreary years for someone who she claimed was more passionate but who, despite that, still kept in touch with him, sometimes literally, when he asked her to do so.

He had realized too late that she had meant more passionately giving rather than more passionately demanding. Was he looking for another woman who would love him and leave him? It couldn't be that. It had taken him long enough to get over Jilly. Whatever it was, he had never found it. Maybe it wasn't to be found. It might not even exist. It might be a need that could never be satisfied. He had tried but always failed. It was the story of his life. There had been plenty of needs but very little fulfilment.

He took out his phone and looked at his favourite picture. It was of a dog swimming in a rough sea. It was totally alone. The dog was desperately trying to keep its head above water. The artist seemed to have painted it in such a way that anyone looking at it would realize that the outcome for the dog was inevitable. Silas regarded it as more of a self-portrait than as an example of the artist's fondness for animals. He thought of his sculpture, of all the beautiful boys that he had created with love and which everyone admired but hardly anyone bought. Were they self-portraits? Was there something he had put into them that ensured the inevitability of their being rejected? He loved his bronzes. He loved beautiful boys.

He had been sculpting cherubs for most of his adult life, but this was the first time he had admitted to himself that he loved boys. He felt shocked. Loving boys was a dreadful problem. He could go to prison. He could be put on the Sex Offenders Register. They might want to tag him electronically. Silas found himself creating a situation in which he could only be a victim. It was like being with Jerry or Benedict. He was dimly able to recognize that his imagination was giving him a hard time when he didn't deserve one. He resolved to find out from his therapist why he was so afraid of authority and of criticism – although he thought he knew the answer to that one. But how could he stop it? He might also talk to her about how he felt about beautiful little boys.

EIGHT

❧

Alex and Lola left the theatre with mixed feelings about King Lear and his daughters. Lola felt that the King was right to ask them to make a public declaration that they loved him before leaving everything to them in his will. Alex did not.

'It's wrong for a father to blackmail his daughter by threatening to withhold her inheritance unless she pleases him,' she said. 'In fact, it's disgusting. Cordelia refused to go along with that. She stuck to her guns. She knew he should have loved her whether she pleased him or not.'

Lola was puzzled by how strongly Alex felt about it. 'What's so important about that?'

'It's demanding, for a start. It's wrong for a parent to do that. You never know where pleasing a father might lead.' After pausing for a moment she said, 'How would it be if he expected her to please him sexually?'

She wondered why she had said that. Her thoughts went back to her mother's death. Where was her father when she needed him? He may not have physically exploited her, although she often wondered whether her memory impairment had blanked it out. But by using her as a crutch after her mother died he had certainly exploited her psychologically. If he had been more available would her brother have tried to behave as he did, and, if he had, would she have been less reluctant to send him packing? Her father had never been her ally, never been a rescuer. He had sat at his desk in his study all day staring out of the window, thinking only about the loss of his wife. He had never been there for her. He had left everything to her mother including his daughter's upbringing. After her death he had faded so far into the background that he had virtually disappeared.

Lola wasn't sure whether she knew what Alex was going on about, but she didn't want to talk about it. Wondering where pleasing fathers could lead was a long way outside her experience. If Alex had a problem with that she didn't want to hear about it. She didn't even want to think about it. She was four when her parents divorced, an event for which she had always blamed her mother. She might also have blamed her father if he had been around.

Lola had expected Alex to want to talk about her mother again, but after her last comment she was hardly surprised when she began to talk about something else that must have been troubling her for a long time. Going to the theatre had certainly stirred up something. In a voice that Lola hadn't heard before but which made her feel strangely uneasy she began talking for the first time about her emotions.

She began by telling her of an incident that had occurred on the farm on which she had grown up and which she thought she had forgotten. She was almost fourteen, and it was during the summer break. Her father had hired a new farmhand, and sitting beside him on the tractor one early autumn morning, hypnotically drawn to the monotonous repetition of the threshing and the tying of the corn, she had become suddenly overwhelmed by a desire to kill a frantic rabbit as it fled from its soon-to-be demolished home.

She wasn't allowed to use the shotgun but a moment later had persuaded the boy to hand it over. There was something about its destructive power that elated her. It was a power that could be taken up and put down at will, a power which could control and kill, a power which she envied because it belonged essentially to men. The farmer's boy possessed this power. She didn't want to share it with him. She wanted to own it. She didn't understand why she wanted it, but she resented not having it. As she watched the rabbit hopping frantically away from the harvester's mutilating blades, she blasted it with both barrels discharging simultaneously into its head and body. She saw it leaping into the permanency of death. The helplessness of the rabbit and the thought of its gratuitous end calmed her feelings of impotent rage, providing momentarily relief from the ever-present 'why me?' sense of sadness which she had come to accept as an unwanted companion that accompanied her everywhere.

The boy was tall and strong-looking. He was staring at her. She met his eye until he looked away. She had no experience of males – her father and her brother Andrew were the only ones in her life – but she felt that there was something animal-like both in the boy's interest in her and in her growing reaction to him. She could only associate him with the obvious masculinity of the horse her father kept for hunting. She was attracted to his odour, the smell of the stable, the aroma of the farmyard, the sweat of his brow. They were familiar and comforting yet at the same time novel and exciting.

There was a silence. Alex had paused in her account of an event that meant a lot to her. She had never forgotten it. It was a feature of her life. It comforted her whenever she thought about it. It made her feel good. But it remained a reverie, a never-to-be-repeated memory of something so attractive that it had to be forbidden. It was a daydream. She wasn't sure, but she felt that the dead rabbit had stood in briefly for her father, and she thought of how at the same time she was attracted to the farmhand and that even in death there is life. 'I was frightened of my father and often quite angry

74

with him,' she said. 'But he always tried to be nice to me; whenever he was around, that is. I don't think I saw much of him.'

Rethinking her feelings about her father always followed on from the anger generated by his lack of interest in her. She had never been able to cope with the guilt that her failure to observe the demands that the First Commandment invariably generated in her.

'Andrew was always around. It was Andrew I hated.'

She had convinced herself that she didn't know why she had hated Andrew. She tried to remember him, how he had been while she was growing up and particularly just before he died. She told Lola that she had had a dream that she had never forgotten. It wasn't long after her encounter with the farm boy. She had fallen asleep and was dreaming that he was with her and had his arms around her, and she was feeling something unfamiliar but intensely pleasurable. She felt warm and at peace. She slowly and dreamily awakened wishing that he really was there, sitting on her bed, hugging her. But someone's arms *were* around her, someone was sitting on her bed and someone was far too close. She tried to sit up and her brother said, 'Don't worry. It's only Andrew' – and she did worry because it was Andrew. But what she didn't tell Lola was that she had not only thought it was her father but she had wished it had been.

Maybe her father had wanted her to confide in him after her mother died, but she was afraid of how much she craved affection and had pushed him away. She hardly knew him. It was she who had kept him at arm's length. It wasn't the other way around. She was embarrassed by how she felt not because he featured in her dreams but because he featured in her daydreams. Until her death her mother had been there most of the time; usually willing to listen, ready with a hug. Papa had also hugged her sometimes, and she would sit on his lap, and then suddenly it had stopped.

She knew why it had stopped. She had stopped it. She had felt lonely and unwanted for a long time afterwards and didn't know what to do. Did she have a duty to him, a duty to comfort him because he continued to mourn her mother? She could never replace her mother, but sometimes she wished she could do just that. She had lost her mother, but because of her need to be loved had she also lost her father?

'I know he must have been depressed, but I didn't understand that then. I think that after my mother died he was afraid to get too close to me,' she told Lola. She amazed herself by all her rationalizations. Even after all this time she wouldn't allow herself to work out what was true and what was not. She knew only what she feared most was what she wanted most. 'I can see why I desperately needed someone to love me. No mother and a father who wouldn't even put his arms around me because he was worried about his feelings. I didn't know it then. I thought it was because he didn't like me.' She could have added that it was also because she was worried about her feelings, too, but she decided that was enough for Lola to be going on with.

They were both unusually quiet on their way back to the flat they shared over a hardware shop near the Imperial War Museum in south London. They talked for a while about the play, had something to eat and decided to have an early night. *King Lear* had disturbed them both. Although their views about fatherly love differed, each thought they could understand how the other felt. Lola had almost never had a father and seemed to have very little idea of how children were expected to relate to one, whereas Alex's experience of fathering had been shaped by the death of her mother. How much, if anything, did she owe her father in compensation for that loss? The King's words about having a thankless child being sharper than a serpent's tooth seemed to fit both of them.

They asked one another if demonstrable thanks would still have been expected of them if Lola's father had not left before she grew up or if Alex's father had not spent most of her later childhood trying to cope with the loss of his wife instead of looking after his daughter. There seemed to be no answer, but the conclusion they reached was similar. Both had been cheated out of the presence of a strong man in the family. Alex couldn't help wondering who was to blame. It was with a shock that she came to the conclusion that if her mother, by getting herself killed, had not left her in the care of her father whose love for her was at best uncertain she would not be feeling as she did. That she was unable to voice such views with any of the protagonists involved distressed her. Two of them were dead, and the other, she thought bitterly, might as well have been, since he had seldom shown any interest in helping her confront how she had felt then and how she still felt. She felt more helpless than ever. Even after all the years that had passed since her mother's death she was still having problems with the fall-out. Giving one another one of the hugs they had convinced themselves they had missed out on, they went to bed. Alex could not sleep. She had never found it easy to cope with anything to do with missing out.

NINE

❧

It had been a long weekend, and a bank holiday tacked on to the end of it made it seem even longer. The group were pleased to get back to the gym and their friends. They arrived one at a time and gathered in the canteen for a few minutes, either to get their breath back before embarking on their exercises, which they believed were why they turned up so religiously, or to have a look at the newspapers. All had information to share, questions to ask or comments to make. Most of it would wait. Discussion was saved for the post-exercise period. Physically and mentally depleted, they would enter the final stage of the morning, where energy, physical and mental, would be restored through food, drink and conversation.

Jerry and Silas hailed one another amicably, their previous encounter forgotten, possibly to be resurrected later. Harold and Benedict greeted each other, Drago smiled and muttered inaudibly, Luc was late as usual, and finally Lola and Alex, looking particularly elated, arrived and greeted everyone. Encouraged by Luc to get started on the morning's exercises they chatted their way through the treadmills, bicycles and exercise machines and reappeared an hour or so later smelling either of honest toil or of soap with an aroma purporting to be roses.

The gathering began with coffee and tea or whatever soft drink happened to be the flavour of the month. Jerry was drinking a can of coloured water from South America which a Polish work-experience student behind the bar assured him was good for him. Something else was happening, however, which was noticed by just two of them.

Alex, fresh from telling Lola of her encounter with the groom's farmyard odour and unable to put it entirely out of her mind, and Silas, with his preoccupation with the need for someone to love him and no longer satisfied by creating cherubs or with imagining that he loved little boys when he knew he did not, drifted slowly down the coffee queue.

Both were struck by a sensation so powerful that they thought it would sweep them off their feet and throw them to the floor. Suddenly hyperconscious of each another, powerful emotional interactions overwhelmed them. Neither anticipated such feelings nor understood the bizarre images and frighteningly pleasurable and recognizable sensations that began to engulf them. Their body language was a highly emotional non-verbal communication which they imagined everyone else would tune into and in some way criticize.

They were conscious of the absence of emotional space between them. Neither knew what to do. Alex experienced the conflictual sensation of wanting to run and of wanting to stay, of longing for something but being afraid of what she longed for, and Silas found himself frozen into immobility and into speechlessness. Discussing it later, they discovered that they had experienced a familiarity with one another that was so intense that they were certain that they had met somewhere before, in another place, in another time, in another existence.

Silas felt that he was speed-dating at a pace so fast that he thought he would collapse. He was in a panic and not sure why. He couldn't deny that he was aroused, and he was embarrassed. He realized for the first time that the group was his family. Were they the brothers he had never had? One of them might even be the father he had never known. What he felt about Alex must be wrong. Alex was a sister, a daughter. He prayed that no one had noticed what was happening to him. But what if they were talking about it? Jerry was very perceptive. Might he already be commenting on it?

He had seen Alex before and never felt like this. Why now? Of whom or what had he been reminded? Was it something or someone he had known? Was she one of his cherubs, a female one? Was she an angel? No, she was not an angel. He didn't want her to be an angel. Angels were too feminine, too fragile. Angels needed caring for. She was very young. Was she too young? But she was boyish. That was a plus. His emotions besieged him. He thought he might faint. Everything around him, except Alex, seemed unreal. He could see her clearly. He had never believed in halos, although he might have created one occasionally for a particularly attractive Cupid, but Alex seemed to have one. Was he thinking of Cupids or of cupidity? There were no female Cupids. He didn't know what he was thinking about, and he suddenly realized he didn't care. His only identifiable thought was that someone seemed to want him. Nothing else mattered. He had never been wanted. Had he been attracted by her perfume? He thought of his mother. She had never wanted him. It could have been her perfume.

He tried to ignore Alex. He must be imagining what was happening. He smiled at her politely as if he knew her from somewhere. He looked around him. He forgot about the coffee. He had to talk to someone. Benedict was hovering. Silas walked purposefully towards him as if he had forgotten something.

Benedict said, 'There's a queue . . .'

'I have to talk to you. It's important.'

Benedict looked worried. He didn't want to talk about anything important. It was a word girlfriends used when they wanted to talk about marriage and babies. His present one had said something of the sort when he left that morning. He had been pleased it was a gym day where issues cropped up but no one ever spoke about resolving them. He was about to say that he had to dash. He opened his mouth to tell Silas that he had an appointment with his doctor. It was too late. His companion took his arm and walked him towards a quiet corner. No one noticed them. Benedict found himself torn between his wish to know nothing of Silas's problem and curiosity about what it could be. When Silas began talking he knew that he would be in for a long haul. He looked surreptitiously at his watch.

'I never knew my father,' Silas said to Benedict, who wondered why he seemed to have begun in the middle of a sentence. 'He left when my mother was pregnant. When she was angry with me, she would tell me that if my father had said he was leaving her before it was too late for an abortion I would never have been born. She was often angry with me. Probably all the time, I expect. She was a hairdresser in a salon miles away from anywhere. She collected me from the childminder on her way home each day. I remember waiting for her. She was always late. She never had time for me. I thought one day she would forget to come and the childminder would put me in the street and close the door.'

Silas began to feel sorry for himself. He hoped that Benedict hadn't noticed that his eyes were moist. Thinking about his mother always made him feel sad. It was worse when he spoke of her. It was as if he could see her, touch her. He had always wanted to touch her. He did occasionally touch things that reminded him of her. The feel of anything made of wool sometimes aroused him sexually.

Benedict was confused by Silas's sudden account of his early life. He pretended he was not. He could think of nothing to say. The best he could manage was a muttered 'Pretty rotten.'

But Silas wasn't listening. He was in the past with his mother and just wanted to stay there for a while.

Benedict wished he could sit down. He had done the gym. It was their sitting-down time.

'I always tried to please her,' Silas went on. 'I was taken into care for shoplifting when I was seven.' He went on to explain that it had not taken long for the local pharmacist to link the boy who hung around his shop every day on his way home from school with the disappearance of what turned out to be his mother's favourite perfume. Silas barely remembered what she looked like, but he could still smell her perfume.

He suddenly understood what the internet dating was about. Why he had to look first and why nothing ever came of it – because nothing in his life had ever come of anything. Not least a relationship with a woman. He was looking for someone who would want to be with him and care for him. He asked himself whether such a person existed. He stood there shaking his head.

The now concerned Benedict was relieved when Silas left as suddenly as he had come.

Silas returned to the coffee queue and looked more closely at Alex. She was nothing like his mother, but she did smell like her. It was definitely his mother's perfume, and she was wearing it.

It took Alex a moment to recall where she was. She told herself to pull herself together. That's what it means, she told herself. She was coming apart. She didn't know what to do. It was like the day her mother died. She felt lost, not sad, but disintegrating. It was a paradox of closeness and detachment. What she had been seeking for so long began to overwhelm her. He's come to rescue me, she told herself. He's come to take me away from my past. It was free- dom. She had been locked up for years in an emotional prison serving a life sentence with no time off for good behaviour. They drew together, emotionally closer, but physically apart. Neither of them was sure of anything. Alex worried briefly about what the others might think. Like Silas she wondered whether they could see what was happening. But only she and Silas were in the moment. And then, even more briefly, she wondered how she could even think of getting involved with someone twice her age.

It had happened once before. She had been looking for a job soon after she had left school. She had seen an advertisement for a photographic model in the local paper. She had answered it, knowing that it was not a particularly sensible thing to do. The photographer who interviewed her seemed to be taking more of an interest in her than was appropriate, and she discovered that he worked for an agency that supplied pictures to girlie magazines. She told herself that she could look after herself but knew that her reason for taking the job had been the photographer's interest in her.

He was older than she was, although not as old as Silas. From day one she found that having him photograph her was extra-ordinarily stimulating. She was not exposing herself to the faceless thousands of men who bought the magazines but only to him. It was he whom she was pleasing. The exhibitionist in her had found a voyeur in him, and they were both happy in their need for one another. She experienced his camera as part of him, an extension of him. He saw her as a body to be penetrated and directed his camera in such a way as to gratify his fantasy. His portrait lens brought her close to him. She didn't question him, neither did he her. She was content to conduct their hands-off relationship in her head. She enjoyed being in touch with her powerful look-at-me needs, knowing they were enhanced by his peeping-Tom fantasies. It was entirely selfish, and she enjoyed it all the more because of it. She soon gave it up. No harm had been done to her. Whether she had done harm to her employer she neither knew nor cared. Perhaps that was how she felt about Silas.

She wondered why she was already thinking of an escape route before there was any need. They had not yet spoken a word to each another.

Moving towards the table, they sat down as room was made for them and for their polystyrene cups. No one stopped talking. No one looked up. Alex had joined the group. She had slipped in while no one was looking. She felt immediately embraced. But Silas felt triumphant. He had become a person of substance. He had infiltrated a woman into the group, and his decision had not been disputed. He felt disappointed that no one had noticed it. He wanted to stand up and be counted, to be recognized, to be acknowledged as someone of importance. He wanted to be the leader of the pack, the bull male – or was it the rogue male? But there was no leader. A leader suggested autocracy. The group was a democracy. The pack didn't acknowledge his needs because there was no pack. They were a self-governing collection of friends. They all had rights and exercised them constantly. All were equals.

Silas didn't know how to be an equal. He didn't know about being, only about doing. Neither did he know much about men. The only men he had known were his mother's lovers, none of whom had stayed long enough to make any impact on him other than to strengthen his belief that men came and then they went. He shivered. There was no break in the conversation. No one even looked up.

Alex looked at Lola. She was near by but alone and experiencing a sense of loss so intense that tears had come to her eyes. It was a loss recognized only by her friend, a loss as powerful as Alex's gain. Alex felt guilty and disloyal. She would talk to Lola about it later but not now. She had come home. She was one of the family. She might even have discovered where her mother and her brother were – or at least where her memories of them were.

TEN

Alex and Silas met once a week. They told one another that they would have liked their meetings to have been more frequent, but the pattern suited them. They texted and emailed. Neither realized why the combination of intimacy and distance was so compelling.

When Alex thought what made the nature of their liaison so attractive, she concluded that it was because she was used to the idea that loving relationships were always short-lived and that when coping when the closeness ended abruptly was a frightening prospect. It was not so much that distance lent enchantment, which she conceded it might, but it provided room for manoeuvre. Was Silas another man with a camera?

A girl at school had fallen in love with a television news-reader. Separated by a pane of glass, she could look but not touch. He could look but not see. She also must have believed that love was an illusion, distance safer and ultimately less painful. Alex wondered what the pane of glass was that separated her from Silas. She wanted to believe that it was the gap year she was planning that would bring the relationship to an end. It was unexpected endings that she tried to avoid. The fact that the relationship was self-limiting pleased her. But she suspected that there might be other reasons why too close a liaison with someone who loved her was likely to make her feel uneasy. Closeness was all or nothing, with 'all' being forbidden and 'nothing' unbearable. She could not cope with either.

Alone at night she fantasized about her relationship with him, about his compliments, his protestations of love, the places they visited, the exchanging of confidences, the secrets they would keep from the others. She encouraged him to buy clothes and then arranged how he wore them, changing his appearance so that he would look more attractive. She was unable to accept him as he was, and most aspects of their lives, even their sexual involvement was at arm's length and controlled by her. How long, she asked herself, would it be before he also heard the voices in her head constantly reminding her not to become too close?

Silas's daydreams on the other hand were more prosaic. He used seductiveness and compliments to entice Alex into fulfilling his sexual needs. Faceless women and unknown men jostled with one another in his psyche as he re-enacted with Alex his wishes and his hopes. Those that were too violent or too dangerous remained the substance of his fantasies. Unlike Alex, he was less interested in romance and more in gratification. Each looked to the other to compensate them, in ways they didn't understand, for the love their pasts had failed to provide.

Their meetings settled into a pattern. Every Monday and Thursday Alex came to Silas's home where she cooked for the two of them. Their tastes and interests were identical. They liked the same colours, the same leisure activities, the same routines and the same food. Shellfish was a passion. The hard shell of the crab, the claws of the lobster and the struggle to eat the soft flesh that lay within reflected their expectations of each other. Both had been hurt, and both had created armour-plated shells. Neither wanted to be hurt again. They didn't realize that they were also cold fish, but cold they certainly were. As far as taste was concerned they differed only over food that was spicy. She discovered later that his appetite for spice, like his appetite for sex, was in inverse proportion to her own. Alex's responses depended on whether Silas was able to persuade her that she was not only loved but lovable. Silas searched within her for the love which his mother had hidden from him. He enjoyed the search more than Alex.

ELEVEN

৯৯

Harold was walking home. He preferred it to the bus. It took longer, but he was in no hurry. The longer the better as far as he was concerned. There was nothing to rush home for, and soliloquy was safer than conversation and often more interesting. He was thinking back to his birthday lunch. It was not that he had not wanted to spend the money. He had plenty of money – his pension was a good one – it was because he was afraid that they would find out about him. They were all so perceptive, especially Jerry. He knew he had to be careful with that one. Once a detective always a detective. When he decided to investigate something nothing would stop him. Look how he had been when he was carrying on about Billy the Baker. Pretending he might have been murdered. Who would murder Billy? There would be nothing in it for anybody. Not being able to order in a Chinese restaurant. That was a good one. He would have to be careful. Making up complicated stories meant he had to remember them. Why did he say he was an expert on medieval tapestry? He would not recognize medieval tapestry if it stared him in the face. He certainly would not be able to talk about it. If a tapestry expert were to join their group he would have to find another gym. He hoped it would not come to that. He really liked most of them, maybe all of them, even the two girls they seemed to have befriended. He thought the fuss they made the day when that woman came in with her husband a bit put on. It certainly didn't bother him. He could talk to anyone, but he didn't want to. He imagined the shock they would have if they knew who, probably more likely what, he really was. Not because he was a celebrity, because he wasn't, but because he was different; in every possible way.

What were they talking about this morning? He could not remember. He had been tied up with Benedict. Well, not exactly tied up although he would not mind if he was. If any of them would understand him it would be Benedict. He was older than the others, and you could talk to him about anything. Well, almost anything. They had been talking films. Old ones on the movie channel in the afternoons. Neither of them liked the films made now. They were too violent. They depicted too much greed, too much ambition, too much dishonesty. The afternoon ones pleased the nostalgic older people and had been made when cinematic gratification consisted in collecting cigarette cards with pictures of film stars on them. They were more to his taste. But what was his taste? He liked women, he certainly liked Sandra, his partner, and his three small boys, but his fantasies were sometimes about men or gay women. He thought he might be gay himself. He liked being with gay men, but he did not want to have sex with them. What he did not like was his penis. It was ugly. He felt its ugliness reflected an aspect of himself he must always keep hidden. He could not look at it or at anyone else's for that matter. He some-times wished he had been born without one.

He had discovered a rare medical condition on the internet called penile something-or-other where about one in 5 million or maybe it was one in 50 million male babies – he could not remember exactly how many – was born without a penis. Surgery had to be carried out to create an artificial vagina so that the child could grow up believing he was a girl. He would then have no doubts as to who he really was. He had no idea who he was. A doctor had once told him that were he to satisfy certain criteria he could be considered for gender reassignment surgery. He had looked it up on the internet. The idea of having surgery terrified him. He did not want to change his gender. He liked himself as he was. He'd had a better idea. He would hide his penis by covering it up. If it was out of sight then it would be out of mind, and he could pretend he did not have one. He had been doing it for years. He had even tried it out on a nudist beach. No one had even noticed. They must have thought he was a woman. No one gave him a second glance. It had occurred to him that they might have been too embarrassed, but he preferred to think it was because they thought he did not have what his mother always referred to as his teapot.

He told himself he did not want sex with anyone. He just wanted to be rid of something he hated. He thought for a moment. That was wrong. He did occasionally want to have sex but only with his penis well out of sight or covered by a notice that would have 'OUT OF SERVICE' written on it in capital letters. He laughed, and a passer-by looked at him curiously.

If any of his friends knew about his preoccupation he would never be able to face them again. It would be too embarrassing. No one could possibly understand it. On the other hand, they might dismiss it. What he liked about his gym friends was their unquestioning acceptance of one another. It was like the nudist beach. All was revealed, but no one saw anything. It didn't seem to matter that however much members of the group exposed themselves and their feelings no one was judgemental. That was why he came. Most people had something to hide. Occasionally topics did come up which one or another of them didn't wish to discuss.

He put on his gym things at home ready to start the exercise class. He would never risk the communal changing room with the others. He didn't want them to see him without his clothes, and neither did he want to see them without their clothes. He might just catch a glimpse of something he preferred not to see. His gym friends accepted him as he was. He did not need to prove anything to them. Sometimes he didn't even bother to wear what he called his heavy-duty underpants when he was with them. There could not be a greater test of acceptance than to be taken as he was. Then he would be able to live not only inside his head but outside it as well. He knew that some people felt the same way as he did about other parts of their body. There had been a woman in his evening class once who was hung up about her nose. She thought it too big and was forever trying to persuade plastic surgeons to change its shape for her. One of them had operated on her, but it had made no difference to how she felt about it. He did not want surgery. He wanted to hide what he disliked about himself and hide the fact that he wanted to hide it.

Benedict didn't like water. Perhaps he was trying to tell people something. Perhaps what he meant was that he did not like taking of his clothes. He might be the one he would confide in. He would understand what it was all about. He was sure there was something Benedict had to cover up, something he needed to conceal. He would find out what it was.

TWELVE

❦

Silas was sitting at home brooding. He and Jerry had a lot in common. Jerry was suspicious of everyone and everything. Guilty until proved innocent. Silas was also suspicious. Not of everyone, only of anyone whom he believed rejected him. He had been distressed when Jerry and Benedict had continued talking when he had turned up the previous month. They had not stopped to greet him. If it wasn't for Alex he would give up the gym altogether. In fact, now that he had her did he really need the others? It would have been different if they had taken him to their bosom. He paused to wonder what he meant by this. He was not particularly attracted to the breast. No breast had ever done much for him. Neither did he like milk, certainly not if it was warm. The thought of it made him shudder. Was he thinking about his mother? When he had wanted her to be around, when he had needed her and couldn't live without her, she was nowhere to be found. Now she seemed always to be with him. He could not rid her from his thoughts.

He thought of a painting that Benedict had admired in the window of an art gallery. A man, a woman and two children sat at a kitchen table over a meal. It was a cosy domestic scene. No hidden meanings, no metaphors. OK, so it was a family and they were eating together and they looked happy and they were in the kitchen. The kitchen was an important place in the home. He knew that. Some psychologists thought of it as the powerhouse, the mother, the place where the food came from to feed the family. Or was it the oven that was the mother? No, the oven was the womb. He hated the expression 'a bun in the oven'. It was distasteful to think of pregnancy in that way. Could that be what he wanted? To start over again with a mother and hope that it would work properly the second time around. Wasn't that what divorced couples were looking for? A fresh start, perhaps with stepchildren? The idea of wanting to be close to any mother, given his experience with his own, was too disagreeable to think about.

Everyone had a role to play in the family. The father brought home the bacon, the mother cooked it and the children ate it. As a student he had lived for a year in New York. He thought of what passed for family life there. Some homes had a cooker with the shelves still in the wrapping in which they had been delivered. Everyone ate out, including breakfast. No wonder the divorce rate was high and kids roamed the streets looking for what might have been provided in their kitchen – if they'd had one. People who prayed together stayed together. His parents had neither prayed together nor eaten together nor done anything together as far as he was aware. Perhaps his life would have been different if they had stayed together. Perhaps everyone needed a bosom. Whether it was to cry on, be comforted by or simply to feed from he was uncertain.

He remembered being annoyed by a gallery owner who almost took on an artist friend of his but then decided not to because he said his work was too 'photographic'. He had thought that that was good about his friend's work. You knew where you were with it. What you saw was what you got. Images you could recognize. There was nothing abstract, cubist, impressionist, postmodern or metaphorical about it. He hated all that stuff. It was the past that preoccupied him.

He would stick with little boys. You could touch them, hug

them, pick them up, put them down, and even leave them out in the rain if you wanted to. He had really enjoyed producing a sculpture once for someone with a large garden. It looked like it was supposed to look; a giraffe, so life-like that in the evening light people actually thought it was real. What he liked about sculpture was that it was three-dimensional and not an illusion like painting. He thought of his studio in the country, of his models, of the feel of the clay, of his kiln and the molten bronze and the beautiful Cupids that evolved from it. That was the reality he longed for.

Was Alex an illusion or was she real? How could he find out? Nothing that had happened to him so far had been genuine. Certainly nothing like what was now happening with Alex. He had craved for a real family when he was a child. A family like he imagined other boys had. He would picture tea waiting when he came home from school and eating at the kitchen table with his mother. He thought of the discussions he had never had with his dad about football. Creating little boys that were lovable and looked like him helped, especially when they were admired by the occasional prospective client who visited his studio. Studying the work of artists who were able to paint their needs on to canvas and seemingly gain satisfaction from doing so also helped, but it could never be enough. He thought of how even the most renowned of artists, whose work fetched astronomical sums, were never really satisfied with what they had achieved. They were all like him. They wanted the real thing. They wanted a real family, real sex and real love in their lives. Reality must always be better than illusion. Having to make do with images created in a studio was second best. He understood why he had needed the family at the gym in whose bosom he felt safe. He did not need that now. The group were no more real than the painting he had seen in the gallery window. Only people who had never had reality had to invent it.

Someone loved him now. He might create his own family with her. It was not too late. Having a child, a boy preferably, would provide him with a second chance. His boy would not grow up like he did with an absentee father and a violently selfish mother. He did not want a symbolic family. He had tried that. He wanted an actual one. But he had done that, too, and that hadn't worked either. His thoughts were running away with him. He had shifted from reality into fiction. A wave of unhappiness swept over him. What on earth was he going on about?

He wondered how Alex would feel about his thoughts. She seemed so like him. How would she react if he told her about his fantasies? Would she feel the same as he did? Would she want a fresh start with him? Could she identify with a child they had created and relive their lives through this child? Would she want to? Their child would benefit by a loving upbringing. It would lack nothing. It would never have to steal love as he had stolen it or be distressed because someone had lost interest in him and turned to another. Everyone he had known had done that. Benedict had done it when he had gone to get the coffee and had not come back.

He returned to thinking about the group. There was something about them he could not quite put his finger on. On the whole, he enjoyed being with them. They were all so different, and yet they were also very much alike. He thought of the group as a rope. Perhaps that was what had attracted him in the first place, despite the occasional problems he had with one or other of them, particularly Jerry. You could get hold of a rope; it was something to hold on to, a support to cling to if there was a problem. He thought about its strands. Its strength depended on its strands. What would happen if one of them left? It would be one strand weaker. It looked strong, but its strength was illusory. That would be a worry.

He now understood what he meant when he thought the

group had taken him to its bosom. He welcomed its support, but he no longer needed it. Alex had taken him to hers. A real bosom had to be better than a metaphorical one. He thought back to when he had left home. He was seventeen and desperate to go to art school. He had always been keen on sculpture. It was pottery then. He still preferred clay to stone or marble. You could work with it more easily. 'Like clay in his hands' or was it putty? It gave him a good feeling. The arts teacher told him that he was good at pottery. At the time he believed that he had said that because he felt sorry for him. He preferred to think it was because he was far-sighted. Was he manipulative? He probably was, at least in his wish to create something to which he was entitled. He had never achieved anything simply by waiting for it to happen. Stealing the perfume for his mother, at least had achieved something – or so he thought.

It occurred to him that the reason he was irritated when he was asked to sort out someone's computer problem was not because he felt exploited by them but because he envied them their normal childhood. They never had to do everything themselves. There were always parents around to do things for them or at least help them.

He was awarded a bursary and thought at the time that his mother seemed sad to see him go. Had he imagined that as well? Had she ever loved him? She had never had any time for him, yet he did love her. He and his mother were like the gym group. Neither could have existed without the other. If they were not together they would not be bound to one another. Unbound, they were no longer a rope; more like two pieces of string or a rope with only one strand. They would not last long. They must have needed one another, although neither of them had ever admitted it. Or was it wishful thinking on his part?

He had sensed what his mother wanted when he was quite

young. He was about twelve when he realized he was the only man in her life. In reality there were many, but none had stayed with her. She was too difficult, too demanding. Stealing the perfume had convinced him of his need to be part of another person's life. Perhaps everyone needed that. Alex was a strand, but so was he. Together they could become a rope.

THIRTEEN

Alex was lying in bed with her eyes closed. It was a Silas day, but she was not yet ready for it. She was locked into a dream that was so fresh in her mind that she thought it was still happening. Was it a dream, or was it real? In her half-asleep half-awake state she was afraid that it would disappear were she to open her eyes. She did not want it to disappear. She wanted it to go on for longer.

In the dream she had telephoned a man, a stranger, someone she didn't know but who nevertheless seemed familiar. Why had she phoned him? She tried to remember. She didn't know. She had done it on an impulse. Had they met before? She couldn't be sure of that either. But she was sure that she wanted to speak to him. He seemed to know her, and she was pleased that no introductions were needed.

'You are amazing,' he said. 'You are my ideal. Your eyes, your hair, your body, everything about you.'

Alex did not mind that he was addressing her body. She thought it normal. Men spoke to women's bodies. She wanted him to speak to her body. She was pleased that she didn't know him. She couldn't think of anything to say to him, but that didn't seem to matter. Her body was speaking for her. He was taking responsibility for everything. It had nothing to do with her. Even though she had not said anything she knew she was flirting with him. She felt it safe to flirt because he was someone who did not know her. She felt safe because he was a stranger. Although it was like rape it was not unwanted. Even in the dream she wondered how rape could ever be wanted, but then if it were rape it couldn't be her fault.

He would have no axe to grind. He would give her what she craved and would expect nothing in return. She wanted a gift without strings – not an investment that she would have to repay with interest later.

She was in a car, and they were hungry. They were on their way to a café. They read the menu and waited to order. She knew what she wanted. It was not food. She was hungry but only for sex. It was not on the menu. She wanted to go somewhere where it was today's special. She was running, and he was running. She was on a roller-coaster or it may have been a train. She had to be on it wherever it was going. Its destination had yet to be announced. The scenery sped by so quickly that she had no idea where they were. They did not speak. She did not want to know what had been or what might be, only what was. There was time neither to discuss the past nor to consider the future. They arrived, and only the present mattered.

They made love as in a black-and-white war movie. He was expected to return to his unit in two hours. He was on active service, and she was on active service, locked in combat but only with one another. She was aware of urgency, of speed, of danger and of feelings that were so intense that thinking them out had to be suspended. Their bodies spoke, but their minds had nothing to say. They had become one.

Moments later Alex, now fully awake, felt guilty. Her first thought was that she had been unfaithful not to Silas but to Lola. She had neglected Lola since what she still thought of as the *coup de foudre* with Silas in the coffee queue. An overwhelming sense of sadness swept over her. She had known Lola for ever. They had been there for one another from day one at their primary school.

It was Lola from whom she sought comfort when her mother died. It was Lola to whom she still turned when her anxieties became too much to bear.

It was only recently that she had appointed Silas to play a role he was probably not up to playing. He needed a mother. She was not his mother. What could Silas give her that Lola could not? The biological differences came to mind, and she hated them. She hated Silas. She fell in hate with him as suddenly as she had fallen in love with him.

Alex's elation disappeared. She could understand why in the dream she felt as if she had been raped. She may have provoked it, but it had suddenly become beyond her control. But it was no longer what she wanted. She wanted to discuss her dream with Lola. She would understand. She could see her face on the day she and Silas had sat with the group in the canteen. She knew what Lola must have felt by her falling for Silas and had pretended not to notice.

Was it because she had been overwhelmed by her acceptance by the group as one of the family, or had she been thinking only of herself? Despite her gender, none of them seemed to think of her as a woman. They behaved as if she was one of the boys. But she was not one of the boys. She was not interested in their acknowledgement of her if they had deluded themselves into seeing her as someone she was not. She became angrier the more she thought about it. She was a woman, and she suddenly realized that in the dream she may have been making love to a man but she had thought of him as a woman. The woman was Lola, and whatever the group might have thought she was not one of the boys and neither was Lola.

She continued to feel angry. It was down to her how she thought of herself. She refused to be assigned to a gender to which she did not belong. Perhaps she did think of herself as male sometimes. But it was when she wanted to be in charge. It was only then that she might see herself as having a penis – if only a metaphorical one. None of the others knew that. The fact of being experienced by them as male and accepted by them because of it devalued her. She did not accept their evaluation. She might once have been a victim but no longer. She did not need what they had to offer. When she wanted to feel at home somewhere it would be inside her head. She might once have wanted to join the men because she felt she was part of their family and was being excluded. No longer. She might still attend the gym but only to exercise, only to keep fit.

She wanted to tell Lola what she was feeling. She had always explained things to her. Lola was everything to her. She had always been everything. But since Silas she had excluded her. How could she have done that to her best friend? She would put it right. She did not know how, but she would find a way. She climbed out of bed. Lola had gone out. She texted her. 'I x u. Come home.'

FOURTEEN

❧

The two girls were in the grip of something that they could not easily identify. They knew only that it was intensely pleasurable. Neither of them wanted to question it. They wanted whatever it was to be real, not an illusion that might disappear if they talked about it or looked at it too closely. They had the weekend ahead of them and had agreed that they would get their holiday planning out of the way so that they would have as much time together as possible. Their intention was to play tennis the next day and maybe take in a movie. They wanted everything to be normal, so that however or whatever the 'happening' turned out to be would be an unexpected and a serendipitous surprise for them both. They feared disappointment. They knew about disappointment. Alex thought that nothing could be more disappointing than finding that while you were at school your mother had been killed. Thinking back to the look on Lola's face when she realized that she and Silas had fallen for one another and knowing how excluded she felt must run it a close second. Alex knew it was not in the same league as losing your mother, but after a moment's reflection, she thought, it was not all that far removed.

Alex had cooked a chicken for their dinner. Eating it they talked more than usual, got through a bottle of wine and decided to watch football in bed. They both loved football. The aggression of the fans, the violence on the pitch, the passion involved in getting it in and above all the satisfaction of putting one past the goalkeeper. Not putting one over him. That would be too devious. The goalkeeper was an obstruction, always in the way. He was an achievement blocker. All her life Alex had tried to put one past a goalkeeper. Penalty shoot-outs thrilled her. There had always been someone who blocked her. She had always been kept out by her father. He had never encouraged her in anything. Had never even discussed her career with her. No wonder she had opted for theology. She was looking for a God. Someone she could believe in. Her father was a complete nonentity. There was no way she could have believed in him. She vowed that never again would she allow one man to stop her doing what she wanted.

Alex switched on the electric heater in her bedroom and made sure there was enough hot water for an evening bath. She had been neglecting her friend for too long, and she was going to put things right. If Lola was puzzled by her attentiveness she pretended not to be. More puzzling and also slightly worrying, Lola wondered to what it might be a prelude to. Could it be a fond farewell? That was the last thing she wanted. She desperately hoped not. Alex was her best friend. They had always been affectionate, and, apart from when she had fallen in love with Silas and which no one apart from her seemed to have noticed, nothing had changed between them. She loved her friend, and she would find a way to remind her of her feelings.

What would she do if Alex did leave her? She did not even want to think about it. It would be too depressing. They had always been an item. She had thought it would be for ever. Even when they married they would remain bosom friends. But what if Alex was preparing her for the parting of the ways? What if Silas had really come between them? There were too many imponderables. She tried to put them out of her mind. How they found themselves in one another's arms in Alex's bed, a family heirloom, neither of them knew. The football played on, but they were not watching it. No longer spectators, they were on the field. The only players and in the same team. Although they were playing at home it was not a game. This time it was real. Taking off her pyjamas Lola put her arms around Alex and kissed her. Now on autopilot with restraint thrown aside, they clung to one another wishing that this moment, the happiest they had ever experienced, would last for ever. Alex smiled to herself, slightly anxiously but only for a moment, as flickering across her mind she realized that she was in her parent's bed in a state of arousal with someone who loved her.

There was something about Lola's strong young body that made Alex feel safe. It provoked images of caring and bonding that were non-threatening and loving. There was nothing sharp and pointed or intrusive about it. It was round and accepting, smooth and enclosing. She moved closer to Lola, tracing the outline of a breast with one finger, locating and then identifying a long-forgotten source of comfort, gently enclosing the nipple with her mouth and experiencing such a sense of drowsy fulfilment that she would have fallen asleep had Lola not spoken. Her fiery kisses, her smothering embraces and an orgasmic response of such intensity shortly overwhelmed them. All thought of sleep obliterated, they were miraculously at one and it was more than an hour before they slowly drew apart, but their need for one another continued to unite them.

'Do you think we are in love?'

Alex thought of her mother and for a moment was afraid to answer. Being in love with someone in her experience had always been a prelude to loss. After a moment she said, 'Of course', and, wrapped up one with the other, they eventually fell asleep. Alex had a dream in which her mother appeared, and her mother hugged her and said she loved her, but her mother did not look like her mother but like Lola, and Alex cried in the dream because it was as if her mother had returned.

FIFTEEN

Had anything ruffled the feathers of the group when they had last met it was not apparent. Silas, probably because he thought that Alex was now available to attend to his sensitivities, had finally got over feeling offended by Jerry's delay in acknowledging him that day – although he would have been mortified had he known that it was the same day that Alex and Lola had made love. Jerry had yet to appear, and Drago, who was the first to arrive that morning, said he thought Jerry might have said he was going away for the weekend.

Luc was not his usual self. He was thinking about a fashionable restaurant he had passed on his way to the gym. That the menu read well did not impress him. It had to eat well. What distressed him was what was being unloaded from a refrigerated container truck. Packages of ready-peeled hard-boiled eggs, sealed packs of duck breasts, lamb chops, fish and smoked salmon and containers of potato wedges. All assembled in a factory and probably all frozen. Customers were most likely being told that the fish was 'the catch of the day', and he imagined them opting for 'today's specials'. All phoney, all lies, all total misrepresentation.

Why was he so worked up about it? Most run-of-the-mill restaurants did the same. Being imaginative was all very well, but stretching things to the point of dishonesty was not. Luc looked at the others. Had he been any less dishonest with them? Was he pretending to be something he was not? Misrepresenting himself?

He might be. He could not be sure. The group seemed to have taught him to think about what he was saying. What was he saying? Everyone had to put on some sort of front. Total openness was not always attractive.

Anyway it made him angry that people should be asked to pay good money for so-called fresh food that an in-house chef had only to defrost. Yes, they would have a chef, but all he would be asked to do would be to warm up the customer's order, put it on a plate and smother it with sauce from a catering bottle. The only customers who could possibly enjoy it would be those whose taste-buds were so impaired by drinking too much cheap wine while waiting for their order to be plated up that their judgement, should they have had any in the first place, would be as anaesthetized as their palates.

He thought of his upbringing in France, of his home in the village in which he was brought up, of his parents' restaurant in which all the family worked. It was so different from what he had just seen. The family lived upstairs. His parents did the cooking, and, while he was growing up absorbing the cooking smells from the kitchen and watching meals being created which people would come from miles around to eat, he learned about food. Their food was fresh food. When someone ordered chicken they got chicken because he was sent in to the back garden to kill one. That was fresh food; not the flavourless contents of a packet that was offloaded from a freezer truck. The idea of serving customers with a thigh and a breast from chickens that had probably never even met one another distressed him. It was disrespectful. He was aware that it was not the right word, but it was definitely in bad taste in more ways than one.

He knew what people liked. He had been a people-pleaser all his life. He was particularly proud of his parents' restaurant and even prouder that he had helped them as a teenager, however marginally, achieve its excellence. His father was French and his mother Greek, and he had learned to cook the way his father did. But it was his mother's cooking that had made the greatest impression on him. His mother fed her family for love, while his father fed his restaurant customers for cash. He was fortunate in having parents who cared about food and cared about him. What would his mother, whose lovingly crafted pasta was in his opinion worthy of several Michelin stars, have thought about fast food?

Apart from her intuitive style and her concern for her children's well-being his mother loved to sing. She was happy in her work and sang while she cooked. Her voice and her family were all that interested her. Luc had grown up in the knowledge that the food that went into the mouth and the music that came out of it were of equal importance. His mother spoke well of everyone, and he learned that from her also. When he explained to his friends at the gym how to make a cassoulet or when to drink a Bellini, he was also, in his mind at least, not only singing his mother's praises but hearing her mellifluous voice.

Luc was naturally consulted when deciding where to have one of their birthday lunches. Being the first to offer to buy the coffee each week seemed to be a natural extension of his concerns and responsibilities. He was also the one to whom everyone brought their troubles, and he was pleased that they turned to him whenever caring was on the menu, just as he had turned to his mother to help him with whatever problems he'd had while he was growing up. He missed his mother. She had lived to a great age, and there would never be anyone to replace her. He recognized that there was a lot of her in him. She lived on because he cooked like she did. He remembered her by being her. Like her he was never offended and seldom irritated. He played a caring role with his friends and knew that they admired him for his generosity of spirit. His greatest ambition was to cook for them, but so far he had not been able to persuade a friend to lend them his kitchen for a day.

On his way back from the coffee queue he found the group talking about Benedict who was regarded with affectionate curiosity by the others. They knew that he took his exercise responsibilities more seriously than any of them. He was the subject of a discussion on health that morning because his way of doing things set an example to which they all aspired but few were fit enough to follow. He was working out somewhere in the gym but not with any of the others, because he started at least an hour before they did, exercised for two hours rather than one and joined the group later.

Exercising alone was his passion. They all accepted it and never thought of questioning it. He was somewhere where he could not be seen. An abstentee helmsman was something they all thought of as normal. It was a little-used area of the gym where he could be neither heard nor seen. He wore headphones and listened to the music he loved.

Jerry, who had just arrived and caught the tail end of a discussion on whether Benedict's exercise style really was as good for the heart as he believed it to be, made an intentional conversation-stopping contribution.

'To my mind, the reason he doesn't want anyone to see him is because it's all about you-know-what!'

No one replied because none of them had an opinion. They might well have thought of one if Jerry had given them a moment.

Instead he continued speaking. 'After all, what he does is a do-it-yourself gratification carried out in private. Wouldn't want anyone else about.' Warming to his theme he went on, 'Especially not women. Perhaps no one has asked him, because we might all be as embarrassed about it as he is. Perhaps some of us feel the same way but won't admit it.'

Silas, who thought that Jerry was being even more over the top than usual and forgetting that he used innuendo when he wanted to draw attention to himself, said rather pompously, shaking his head in a schoolmasterly way as he did so, 'He might just be a bit self-conscious.'

He made it sound as if it were he, rather than Jerry, who was the ultimate authority and that his comment had been based on a thorough study of the literature on privately performed gymnastics. That no such literature had been researched by him, even were it to exist, made him wonder why he had taken on a holier-than-thou attitude to Jerry's comment. It must be because it might have something to do with sex. Silas wondered if it had anything to do with Alex. He told himself that he must try to be less pretentious.

Silas could hear Jerry and the others still talking, but he had faded them out. He began thinking about how concerned he was about the girls; both of them, not just Alex. It did not take long for him to realize why he was so worried about their well-being. Women had to be protected against male predators. It was his mother again. Would he ever grow out of the sick relationship he had with her? Should he have taken greater care of her? He was becoming confused as to where his duty lay. He had always wanted to please his mother. He had never given up trying. It had had no effect whatsoever on how she had behaved towards him, and anyway surely it was her duty to love him. He knew she wouldn't have loved him whether he had been pleasing or not. Nothing ever changed the way she had felt. He was an unwanted leftover; a reminder of how she had been treated by men in general and by his father in particular. It was an event that had so impressed itself upon her that her life, and by extension his, would be for ever coloured by it. She had not been able to punish his father. She had punished him instead.

Alex had told him after she had seen *King Lear* that the King should not have demanded that his daughter announce publicly that she loved him. He should have loved her whether she pleased him or not and that the same should have applied to his mother's attitude to him while he was growing up. That was all very well, but she did not know his mother.

He was trying to please Alex, but going on past history he was not likely to be any more successful with her than he had been with any other woman. None of them had time for him. They didn't love him and leave him. They hadn't loved him in the first place. He must have been born unlovable. What a terrible thing to happen to anybody. No wonder he felt compelled to check out the truth of his belief with one woman after another in the hope that he had been mistaken. Depressive thoughts overwhelmed him. What hope was there for him?

Perhaps his relationship with Alex would rid him of the black cloud that was blocking out any chance of happiness. Sex with her had been good, but it had disturbed him lately. He looked around the room to see whether she was near by. He was so conscious of her intuitive ability to tune into his thinking he was sure she would know where his thoughts were taking him.

Would he ever be happy? He could be were he to find someone who genuinely loved him. Perhaps he should give up his demand for sexual gratification and try to be more concerned for his partner's needs. He looked for variation, but it was always based on one theme, the certainty of rejection. Making love to Alex with her back turned was the position with which he had no problem probably because the concept of a woman turning away from him was so familiar. Alex had told him that being unable to see him made sex enjoyable for her but for a different reason. She told him that not seeing what was going on allowed her to disclaim any responsibility for it. It made her feel less guilty. She could not be blamed for anything that went on behind her back. Neither could he be blamed for the way he experienced love. It was not his fault. The only way he had been given what had passed for love as a child was not with his mother for ever moving further and further from him but by never being close to him. He believed that even if she had not had a job outside the home she would have invented one. Perhaps Alex had sensed that and understood it.

What he did worry about was whether it was he that Alex was turning her back on or on sex? What if it was him? He could not bring himself to ask such a question. It might well bring to an end something that, despite his concerns, he was enjoying. In the meantime he had to assume that their chosen style of love-making reflected their wishes and satisfied their expectations. All of it was on the cards that life had dealt him. Maybe he should accept it and not try to change the way he played them. He would try in future to let the cards fall where they may.

There was another thing about Alex that really puzzled him and about which he was longing to talk to her. Not only did she insist that he lie on his side behind her during intercourse but she complained that she was unable to climax unless she gripped his upper leg tightly between her thighs. It might have pleased her, but it prevented him from moving. He did not like what she was doing. He felt trapped. She had taken charge of his feelings. She was robbing him of something that was uniquely his. For a moment he thought not just of the abstraction of maleness but of the reality of his masculinity. Was that what she was doing? Was she trying to steal it from him?

Alex had told him she felt guilty about sex, but he did not know what she meant. Did she mean guilty about playing the woman's role. Did she think she would feel better about it if she were a man? That might be a good reason for wanting a penis. But he was certainly opposed to her having his, whether symbolically or not. He was beginning to wonder if there was something in what he was thinking. He was not entirely convinced that his interpretation of her sexual preferences was correct, but the more he thought about it the more it seemed to him to have in it more than just an element of truth. He could understand that Alex might have a good reason for denying herself the female role if she believed that there was very little future in being a woman. Her brother had been killed in a road accident, and she had told him that she had envied his status in the family. Was she a tomboy when she was a child? Had she now become the boy she might always have wanted to be? Her mother had died in the same accident. She probably had not been much older than Alex was now. If he were in Alex's shoes he might see life in much the same way, but not, he reminded himself, if it was his penis that she seemed to want. After reflecting on the circumstances that they were in and which continued to puzzle him he thought Do I really need this?

He recognized such thoughts as a feature of what life used to be like before he had noticed her. He would then have taken the view that it was time for some more internet dating. Was that what he wanted to do now? The more he went over it in his mind the more attractive it seemed. He had always thought of it as a failsafe fall-back position if things really went wrong with whomever he was with at the time.

The group was listening to Luc explaining how to make a perfect tiramisu and Drago saying that if they all had it for breakfast on gym days they would not need exercise to give them the pick-me-up they required. Those who knew what he was talking about smiled, the others looked puzzled.

Silas paused in his daydreams for long enough to say, 'Lost in translation', a reminder to the others that he was still there and also that he knew the meaning of *tiramisù*, and then returned to thinking about Alex and what was going on in their relationship and thinking how much he used to enjoy internet chat rooms and, even more so, internet dating. Perhaps it was commitment that was so worrying. It had never worked for him. He didn't even know what it was. Even if he saw it he probably wouldn't recognize it. After a moment or two he decided that thinking about his problems with Alex and with women in general was upsetting him too much, and he returned to listening to what the others were talking about. Jerry was still theorizing about Benedict. Luc and Drago were baffled by Jerry's reasoning and were thinking of starting their work-out, and Corker, who had just arrived, listened for a moment or two, then waved his walking stick at them as his contribution to the discussion and announced, 'My voice is in my sword!' and wandered off to the changing-rooms before anyone could ask, although they might have guessed what he was on about.

Jerry took a keen interest in anyone whose behaviour he could not understand. Ignoring Corker's eccentric conversational technique (which they were all used to and only occasionally commented on), he decided that Benedict was concealing something from him. He was puzzled by Benedict, although his suggestion about exercising in private was not entirely serious. He knew that what he had said was more for effect, more to impress the others with his knowledge of the human condition, than because he had any particular view about it. He knew no more about it than they did, but he felt that there were certain expectations he had to live up to.

But Benedict did seem to be living in another world to everyone else. There was something going on that he did not want to discuss. He must try to work out what it was. None of the others seemed interested in discovering why Benedict danced on his own as a way of keeping fit rather than joining in the class aerobics.

Harold, who had just arrived and had listened for a moment to the discussion about Benedict, was looking forward to when he might one day be able to discuss his own problem. He was not yet ready for that. He would, for the time being, try to keep such thoughts to himself, so he said nothing.

Neither had any of them followed up on Jerry's comments on Benedict. Jerry was unable to control his resentment. The group was not interested in his views. He definitely felt left out this morning. He might try again with Harold.

'Why do *you* think he does it'? Jerry said, pushing the Benedict boat out again.

'Does what?' said Harold – not because he did not know what Jerry was asking him about but because he wanted a moment to think about whether the question concealed anything sinister. He decided after Jerry had repeated the question that it did not. 'It's good exercise. A bit like swimming.' He wondered why swimming had come up again. He remembered thinking that the reason Benedict always said that he disliked swimming was not because he did not want to get wet but perhaps it was because, like him, he did not want anyone to see him in the shower afterwards. Anyway since the gym did not have a pool such a possibility was clearly a non-starter. He sighed. 'Too much to hope for.'

'What are you talking about?' Jerry enquired, bemused.

'Nothing. I was thinking of something else.' Harold was on the verge of panic. He had nearly given himself away. How on earth had he let that slip out? He smiled at how his thinking was trying to turn something deadly serious into a joke. Or maybe he wanted it to slip out. He had been hiding it for years. Perhaps he wanted everyone to see it at long last. Did he really want that? No, he certainly did not.

He tried to bring the conversation back to Benedict before

he said something on impulse, intentional or otherwise, he was sure to regret later. 'Benedict told me only the other day that he thinks being constantly on the move is what keeps him healthy. He says he never sits if he can stand. He runs up the stairs two at a time. If anyone offers him a seat on a bus he always refuses, and dancing, walking on his hands, frequent sex and doing everything quickly are what he thinks everyone should aim for.' Benedict had not said frequent sex. Harold had added that to give what he had said more impact. 'What I like particularly about Benedict is his concern for others,' he added. 'I've noticed that he does one exercise, usually when there is no one around, that I've never seen before. He said that he is strengthening his back muscles so that should he come across someone marooned on the wrong side of a narrow ravine he would be able to lie across the gap and then whoever it was could walk across him to safety on the other side. We all aim for fitness, but Benedict is a natural rescuer.'

He was about to say that he wished he would rescue him from his dilemma about whether he should discuss his problem but decided not to at the last moment. Murmurings began to break out. They were not clearly expressed, but it was obvious that Harold's information met with everyone's approval.

Luc was still thinking of restaurants that represented themselves as something they were not. He was also worrying about what it was that he might not have been completely up front about. It had come to him that morning. After a restless night he had realized what it was. He knew that everyone thought of him as a man of integrity. He had convinced himself that nothing could be further from the truth. He felt he had better tell the group about it. It was something that was often on his mind. It might make them change their mind about him. He waited for a moment in case someone said something which might give him an opportunity to bring the subject up. He thought Harold looked as if there might be something else that he wanted to talk about. But he remained silent.

Luc began to explain that when he was around eighteen he had got fed up with the business-management course his parents had talked him into and on impulse had run away and joined the French Foreign Legion. After about a month of sadistic bullying, terrible food and constant talk of colonial warfare in which he was not in the least interested, he succeed in persuading the medical officer that he was unfit to carry out his duties. The doctor confirmed what he had told him, and he had been discharged. He had always been embarrassed by his giving up on the French army so soon after joining it and had been unable to tell anyone a story that he imagined would undermine their views about him. He looked anxiously at his friends.

To his surprise the others seemed to think he was a hero. Although what he had done might have been brave in one sense, if others saw him as a hero he could only see himself at best as a flawed one. Ever since he had left he had thought he should have stuck it out. He could have been a real hero of one of the many campaigns fought by the French in remote parts of what used to be the French Empire instead of a phoney hero valued only by wishy-washy left-wing pacifists. He looked at his friends in whose eyes he had clearly risen a notch or two, while his thoughts flickered over the various wars in Indochina, Algeria, Chad, Ivory Coast and the French parts of Central Africa in which he had missed out. He had missed his chance to prove himself as a soldier despite realizing now that was the last thing he had wanted. He had never told anyone that he had thought of himself as a wimp apart from his gym friends. He felt better for having told them. He smiled very slightly but not enough for any-one to notice. He was happy.

Harold was also pleased that Luc had told them about the Foreign Legion. He admired the man for having the courage of his convictions. He was certain that he was not only brave but sensible for leaving war zones where issues that could more sensibly be addressed by debate were being made worse with guns. He wished he could do the same with his issues. Come to think of it, he wouldn't have been there in the first place. Luc had taken a view about a lifestyle that was not only disagreeable but murderous. Fighting African freedom fighters was hardly noble soldiering. He thought that Luc had a duty to the country that he had agreed to fight for, even though he had clearly acted on impulse. He certainly did not blame him for giving up on that idea. He must have thought that he was leaving his warm, loving family for another one. He could not have been more wrong. It was no wonder that it had taken so long before he had told anyone about it. Everyone has something they want to keep covered up. Such an idea made him feel good. He decided that Luc as well as Benedict might one day be someone that he could confide in.

SIXTEEN

❦

Alex could not remember being so confused. She had really burned her boats. What did she want? She knew the answer before she had finished asking herself the question. She had used Silas to discover whether what she was looking for was something her father had withheld from her, and she had checked out with Lola if what had been lost to her for ever by the sudden death of her mother might possibly be found with her. It couldn't be right to use people to try to find out what had gone wrong in the past or at the very least shed light on it. Wouldn't Lola feel that she was being exploited if she were told that all Alex was looking for was information about how she had been treated as a child by her parents? And what about Silas? How would he have felt if he knew that she was trying to discover whether being loved by an unloved man with a neglectful upbringing would be fulfilling enough to satisfy her need to know that her father, notwithstanding suffering a grievous loss himself, had really loved her, despite having turned away from her? Wasn't that what therapists were for? No wonder people sometimes fell in love with their therapists and wanted to have some sort of involvement with them if they thought they were stand-ins for neglectful parents. Silas had become her therapist for the time being. Anyway, wasn't the entire group therapeutic? She knew that she had not really given up the search for his stand-in. All she had done was replace Silas with Lola. She decided that she was not using them if all she had been doing was taking a

118

fresh look at the information reflected in her interactions with them. Using was not the same as abusing. She did admit, after reflecting for a moment, that sometimes it can be very close.

She did not want to blame her father for his shortcomings. Neither did she want to blame all men for what one man had failed to give her. Her father had been as devastated by her mother's death as she had been. Throughout the time she had lived at home with him he could think of little else. She sighed. He should have made more of an effort to fulfil his motherless daughter's needs. It was too late now, but she was pleased that she was beginning better to understand her misfortunes and her reactions to them.

She recalled the occasion when she had invented the incident in which she had fantasized that her father was indeed making more of an effort to show her that he loved her. It was the night in which she had convinced herself that he was too close to her physically, although she knew that it was her adolescent brother and not her father who had been responsible for that. It had taken her a long time to accept that she had persuaded herself that it was her father, because she wanted to believe that it was him. She was horrified now to think that she had wanted her father to be so close. But, on the other hand, if she'd had a father who was generally concerned with her well-being and had given her a hug from time to time she wouldn't have had to rely on false memories.

She seldom allowed herself to think of her mother in that way. Now so many years after her death she could not bring herself to blame her for anything. She had loved her mother, but she had never been entirely sure that her mother had loved her – at least as much as she loved Andrew. She had thought that she might find out one day. She would never find out now. When she did think of her it was always because of her doubts about whether she as her only daughter was worth loving. Things could have been so different if she had been able to believe that she was as loved as she imagined Andrew had been. She had desperately wanted her mother to see her as Juliet, wanted to show her that someone loved her, even if it was only a character in a play. The only love she could be sure of was Lola's. She knew how Lola felt. But, however much she may have wished it, it could never be the same as having a mother's love.

Whatever spontaneity there had been in the few relationships she'd had in the past, it always ended by becoming one-sided. She was always too controlling. No one really wanted to know how they should behave towards her before she could be convinced that their intentions were genuine.

She did not want to be remembered as someone who could never be satisfied with what is, because what was always ended in disappointment. Most men could be excused for not wanting to live up to such expectations. Most of them, probably sooner rather than later, would decide to call it a day. She was reminded of how she felt about the boy driving the harvester. She remembered her obsessive need for him. Was it love she had wanted, or was it power? Did she want him or the gun? She thought of her insistence that she use his shotgun to shoot the rabbit. With the gun in her hand she became his equal. She was the boy she wished she had been; the boy who would have been loved because there would have been no Andrew to come between her and her parents. No Andrew to exploit her needs. No wonder she felt so guilty when he was killed. She would have killed him herself if thoughts could kill. He would have been dead long before the accident had killed him.

She could see that her method of trying to find either love or power in a potential partner could not possibly work. It made her more confused than ever. She had made promises to Lola that she could not keep, and she was misleading Silas. Was she scapegoating everyone who offered support because her parents had loved her and left her? It was not her mother's fault that she had got herself killed in a car accident, although she could not prevent herself thinking from time to time that it might have been.

She began to reflect on her immediate options as well as her long-term ambitions. Clearly there was no future with Silas, even if he had asked her to share it with him. She had not only gone off him, but as soon as she recognized his weaknesses she had actually begun to dislike him. He was far too fragile and had too many problems. He was still a child. He needed to be the centre of attention and hated it if no one spoke to him for five minutes. Anyway, she had found out that he was married. He had never told any of them. He had been married for about ten years, had a daughter of six and had abandoned his wife immediately after she'd had the baby. The idea of having sex with a mother, despite it being his own child's mother, had horrified him. There was no way he could even sleep in the same bed as his wife. He had thought of it as disgusting. Leaving his child fatherless, as he had been left when his father abandoned him, seemed nothing more than anyone could possibly expect from life.

If she wanted a family and threw in her lot with Lola she would have to find a sperm donor and decide which of them would be the carrier. She sighed. She loved Lola, but she would not be able to cope with that either. It would be too complicated. What she wanted was a family, a home and someone to look after her. She also wanted a career. She could not deny that sex with Silas had been satisfying but only when he complied with her conditions. Sex with Lola was far more gratifying. There were no conditions, but there were a lot of drawbacks. What she really wanted was everything. Was that too much to ask for? She knew it was, but that did not prevent her from hoping that one day she might achieve it.

It was sad that she could not discuss her dilemma in the group. One of them at least might understand how she felt. There was always someone who seemed to tune in to what was going on. Silas would understand because of his problems with his parents, but she could not talk to him about it either in the group or anywhere else. He would certainly not be able to cope with the idea of Lola as a rival. What was it that was stopping her from mentioning it to the others? They were so open about everything. Was it because they were older or male or heterosexual? It seemed more than that. She imagined discussing it with them. There was something about it that felt wrong. It would be like talking to her father about her sexual preferences. She knew how Silas must have felt about sex with his wife. It was too close to home. But she knew what the real reason was. She could have discussed it had she not had an affair with one of them.

None of them was like her father, and then she remembered. They were a family. They were a band of brothers. They were whatever anyone wanted them to be. The group could be a collective parent if that was what they needed. Had they sensed that she had wanted to be a boy and accepted her because of that? They seemed to home in on what was going on even if they were not always sure what it was. Harold was the odd one out. He was obviously male, but it was as if he did not want to be. Neither was he gay. She tried to think why he was not what he seemed, but she could not think what it was.

She had missed out on mothering. She suspected that the group might be a mother. But that was only if she wanted it to be. She was beginning to find her insights quite exciting. How strange, she thought, that she was able to find what she needed by going to a gym. Maybe the others were also able to do that. Physical health she could understand. But mental health. How exciting, she repeated to herself.

Silas must also see the group as a mother but as a mother who at any moment might turn her back on him. She could see why he became so easily upset if the others ignored him for a moment. That was not the kind of mother he was looking for. Others might see the group as a father. She didn't know. They all seemed to have different needs. No point in asking them what she should do. None of them knew what to do. They obviously had not come to the gym to find out, but exploring feelings and finding understanding was an extraordinary bonus to everything else they did there. The brain may not be a muscle, she knew, but hers at least was certainly benefiting from exercise.

She had found out what to do. It had not taken her long. Women were more intuitive than men. She went through them in her mind. Jerry would be hopeless. He was much too intrusive, and she would end up telling him things that were not relevant to her problem. Anyway he was too judgemental. She did not need to ask a policeman for directions. Luc was very caring. She didn't want anyone cooking and fussing over her. She just wanted someone to be there when she needed it. Drago was an unsolved crossword puzzle. Harold reminded her of Lola. What about Benedict?

SEVENTEEN

Benedict had just appeared; showered and looking remarkably relaxed after jogging three miles from his home carrying a heavy shoulder bag followed by a two-hour stint in his 'private' room. He'd had a good idea.

'I know Luc has wanted to cook us lunch for ages.' He looked to see whether Luc and the others agreed with him. They all nodded like MPs sitting near the dispatch box at Prime Minister's Question Time because they knew they were on television.

'But no one will lend me a kitchen,' Luc said.

'That may not be a problem,' Benedict replied. 'I don't know why I didn't think of it before. There's a fairly large yard behind where I have my studio. It's not exactly a garden, although there are a few pots and shrubs in it. It's more like a patio. It would be ideal. There are a couple of tables and some wooden seats and a bench or two and other bits and pieces we could use. If it rains we could eat in the studio. I'm giving it up in a week or two and renting a bigger one. I'm getting more work lately, so I'm joining up with another chap, so it's now or never. I've got plates and knives and forks and a portable cooker. All we'd need is a sunny day and a few bottles.'

Within moments they were discussing menus. Drago, who had recently upgraded himself from being a Croatian waiter to a Belgian minicab driver, suggested mussels, which were eventually dismissed on practical grounds; Benedict's saucepans were not big enough.

They all agreed with Luc's suggestion of avocado and prawns with vinaigrette which he could make at home, and Lola volunteered to cook a daube and heat it up when they arrived.

Luc thought an alternative main course would be an idea for those who preferred something light. 'Curried chicken would be good.'

Drago volunteered to make Bellinis as an aperitif and said he would buy the prosecco and peach juice from the Italian deli near where he lived.

'What's a Bellini?' Harold enquired.

Luc answered by humming the theme from *La Cenerentola*. Everyone was immediately taken with an aspect of Luc of which they had only vaguely been aware. The group's mood, already high, went up another few notches.

Benedict said there was a fridge in his studio and another one in the kitchen, so ice would not be a problem.

Jerry said, 'I'll bring the cigars' – not because he was trying to be amusing but because for a moment he saw himself in another place and at another time.

Benedict addressed Luc. 'Do you think you can oversee all that?'

'Of course I can. I've been overseeing things all my life.' Luc had a mild feeling of regret that the idea he'd had for cooking lunch for the group was being hijacked. He sighed quietly and decided to keep his feelings to himself.

Enthusiasm began to flow like a tidal wave. Pleasurable anticipation was the order of the day, and they began making notes to remind themselves of what they had promised to do.

Benedict could not understand why his idea was meeting with such excitement. He was more into drink than food, although he always enjoyed it when someone else prepared it. His friends were already drunk with enthusiasm. His idea was already beginning to live up to whatever it was they expected of it. 'It's a bit like our group,' he said. 'We're moving into another phase.' And then into a silence filled only by the others wondering what he meant he added, 'Whatever that means.'

He looked at Jerry. He knew he probably didn't know what it meant either, but he would always provide an explanation with such conviction that even though it may have been incorrect others would give it credibility or at least use it as a basis for debate rather than admit they didn't know what he was talking about. It also helped to start the ball rolling.

'My parents often took us on a picnic at weekends.' Jerry said. 'We'd usually head for Southend. Sometimes the traffic would be so bad that we'd get no further than Epping Forest. We used to love going on picnics. It's not like that now. It's tables and chairs and food in freezer bags. My mother would put hard-boiled eggs, a thermos flask, some fruit and sandwiches in her shopping basket and cover it up with a tea towel. There seemed to be more flies around in those days. We'd have a hot cup of tea from a flask and proper cups. Biscuits, too, I think, and then we'd sit in a field somewhere. When we got older it was fish and chips in a café. Life was more of a picnic in the old days.'

'Now,' pronounced Benedict, 'life is a gym.'

They all nodded agreement.

Harold was also enthusiastic. 'Maybe if it's a nice day we could sunbathe.' He thought of the nudist beach and reluctantly dismissed such a thought as inappropriate and said instead, 'It's a pity we can't bring the children.'

'We are the children,' Drago said. 'After lunch we play in the garden.'

Was this the other phase that Benedict was thinking of? Benedict seemed to look over his shoulder while Drago was speaking. He was not sure what he was looking at. Whatever it was it was behind him now. He had a sick feeling for a moment and then a wave of panic. He broke into a sweat. 'It's behind me now.'

Everyone nodded as if they understood. Silas thought that one of the nice things about the group was that everything was accepted. It didn't have to be understood. Explanations were for the stupid, not for the sensitive.

Only Drago had an idea about what he was talking about. He was thinking about his beloved Dubrovnik, the night-after-night shelling, the destruction of his home in the medieval town which once had only Napoleon to contend with in a war which could never have been as bad as the war with Orthodox Christians had been. How they repaired the damage afterwards and put a new roof on his house and how his father and his brother came alive again – but only when he remembered them. 'The past does not always stay in the past.'

'But what if the past has ended and there is a new beginning?' said Benedict.

Benedict looked at Jerry. He was the final arbiter. It was a role he could slip into with very little encouragement.

Jerry thought for little more than a millisecond. 'But when whoever was responsible for the past dies then what? Does his present as well as his future die with him? If he's immortal like Shakespeare then what he's created lives on. Shakespeare is dead, but his creativity is not dead. Only his writing reminds people he once existed.'

Benedict was not convinced. 'You are talking about memory. The talented are remembered by those interested in the words or images they have created. But what about the destructive? After a generation or two they are remembered only by historians. People are frightened of violence, particularly the violent. They deny the existence of violence because it reminds them of their own.'

'Since what people compulsively do in the present is a

reflection of what they did in their past, trying to forget or deny it can't work.' Jerry responded. 'A mountaineer's urge to conquer icy peaks might be a reflection of his efforts to conquer his mother's lack of concern for him when he was an infant. Perhaps she had not provided him with the warm breast he needed but something more like a cold shoulder.'

'Yes buts' were beginning to break out all over the place.

Benedict changed the subject. 'I had dinner with a friend last night. Around ten years ago he was diagnosed with a very rare lung disease, and his heart had more or less packed up. The surgeon said he'd be dead in a month unless a heart-and-lung donor could be found. The donor's organs had to be an exact tissue match with his. You can imagine how everyone on the waiting list felt at having to wait for someone to die so that they could live. It took about three weeks for a heart-and-lung set to become available. Just in time as it happened. Surgeons removed my friend's heart and lungs and replaced them with the heart and lungs from a healthy donor of about twenty-five who'd been killed in a road accident. The operation took hours. During that time my friend was essentially dead. Obviously no one can live without lungs or a heart. Now he's alive again. He was given new life by the surgeon. I was having dinner with a post-mortem male who had once been a corpse. My question is did his past die with him? If I had once been his enemy can I now be his friend, or will he still bear me a grudge?'

Harold's reply, 'Where is fancy bred, in the heart or in the head?' should have wrapped it up, but Drago's 'Do you mean where is fantasy bred?' and Benedict's account of his friend's illness stayed with them.

EIGHTEEN

It was the day of the meal. Luc had gone home after his work-out because his wife had flu and he had to collect her prescription from the pharmacy. He would meet them there. Benedict had been in early and had left about an hour later for reasons unknown, but they supposed it was to tidy up or something, and the six remaining were waiting for the off in the gym. They planned to take a taxi.

Benedict's directions had been rather vague, since he invariably walked and jogged to the gym. He regarded any other form of transport as either for the old and infirm or for the young and lazy.

At exactly 11.45 that morning the remainder of the group stood up, gathered up their contributions to the lunch and went out into the street. They sensed a feeling of purposelessness about themselves that had not been there earlier. It dawned on them that they were waiting for someone to tell them what to do.

'Where does Benedict live?' enquired Jerry.

None of them had thought to ask him, and neither had Benedict thought to tell them. They had all made the same assumption. We are going to Benedict's for lunch so someone will know where he lives. After a few moments' debate ranging from a none-too-serious 'Well, let's not bother then' from Jerry to a more considered 'We could go back to the gym and ask reception' from

Alex, Drago, the only one who had brought his mobile and who had Benedict's number, said, 'I'll ring him.'

In the event they had forgotten to check on how many they were, and two taxis were needed rather than one. Once in them they had time to reflect on something about themselves they had not realized. The group had a uniquely accepting, friendly and dependable persona when they were together in the gym, allowing them to interact well together, but it separated out into its individual components by the time they had returned home. They had no problem as a group because there was always someone to tell them what to do. Now they all seemed like strangers who had never met one another before. They saw the other members of the group in a different light. Not only had they returned to their outside-the-group semi-helpless selves but they were surprised to discover idiosyncratic behaviour in the others that had not previously been apparent.

Jerry had difficulty getting into the taxi because he had backache, Lola had to sit on a fold-down seat because she was wearing a skirt so short that any other kind of seating would have led to embarrassment to others, Silas was angry with himself because he had forgotten to bring any money with him and Harold had to sit on the other fold-down seat because he was wearing underpants that were far too small for him so that leaning back was painful. Alex wanted to be in the same taxi as Lola because she was helping her carry the daube and anyway did not want to be sandwiched between Drago and Silas. They also noticed that no one seemed to be particularly reliable. Only Drago seemed to be his usual self, unchanged and familiar.

Jerry wanted to explain that he thought it was because the others saw Drago as an unknown quantity, since he seldom spoke and when he did it was not always possible to work out what he meant. That allowed them to regard him in any way they wished.

He decided it was not the time to air this observation because they were sitting so close together that anything other than brief conversation would result in an intimacy that would be inappropriate. Also his audience was not at full strength, and he did not want his words of wisdom to be wasted on only a few of them.

The two taxis arrived at their destination simultaneously. Drago, settled now into his self-appointed role as group leader, waved away contributions from the others (except Silas who had not made one) and paid both of them. They found themselves standing outside a large mansion block of apartments which might have been thought of by anyone passing as rather grand. They waited for someone, in his role of the leader, to ring the doorbell. There was no leader.

Drago went to the convenience store on the corner of Benedict's street to buy beer and coke. The others stood casually talking to one another as if either they had completely forgotten why they were there or because they were waiting to be let in despite no one having rung the bell. Had anyone actually done so it would have implied the assumption of an authoritarian role to which none of them had subscribed.

Jerry remembered that being told what to do was discussed one morning by the group, and it was clear that no one liked it. As Harold said, 'We had enough of that while we were growing up.' Doing things by common agreement was acceptable. Being told what to do was not. He realized that what they had in common was dependency. It was one of the things they liked about being a group. Their inability to make decisions was challenged by no one. They expected nothing of one another. They simply went with the flow. Individually none of them could be relied upon for anything, but together they were powerfully supportive of one another's views and wishes. They could be expected to provide expert information on any topic, to listen and not speak, to debate whether the present prime minister was better than the previous one or whether whaling should be banned. Doing something may have been on their menu in the real world, but in the gym nothing more than talking about doing something was expected of them.

The door opened suddenly, relieving them from having to decide what to do next. Benedict had guessed that they must have arrived since they were now almost five minutes later than the agreed time. Punctuality was a measure of their need for security, and he was beginning to worry about where they had got to. He greeted them with a relieved smile and led them through the house at the back of which was what could have been a builder's yard but which was now occupied mainly by a superior-looking shed in which he had his office and the chairs, bench and table at which they would soon be having their lunch.

The sun shone, an oversize golf umbrella to provide shade had been fixed to a cracked chimney pot that looked as if it had been lying in the yard for years, and there was an agreeable smell of cooking. Benedict returned to frying something on a portable gas ring for the first course, and Lola handed him the daube to heat up on the other gas ring for the second.

Drago, now on autopilot, took over when Benedict left to open the door to Luc. 'Wonderful. I love it. What's that amazing smell?'

Luc, now in his element and excited by childhood memories of restaurant life in France, was bustling around Benedict's workplace, turning it in his imagination from agreeable postmodern clutter into, at the very least, a family restaurant. Drinks and food and table settings took on an aura that they did not have before his arrival. Everyone breathed a sigh of relief and the group's usual terms and conditions once more applied. They were invited to wander around Benedict's workshop admiring the projects in which he was engaged while drinking Drago's Bellinis.

Drago was explaining to Lola, 'A really ripe peach should be squeezed in the hand. That way some of the bits go into the glass. Peach juice from a bottle is good – but never from a carton – and only the best prosecco.'

'I'll remember that,' she told him, wondering when she would need this information. Probably never, she thought; not the way things were going. She had no paper on which to write Drago's instructions, but she would try to remember them. She would love a cluttered alfresco lifestyle like this. People, friendly chatter, family life perhaps. She was not sure what that was. She had never had one.

Only Silas felt that he would rather be at home. He was not in the mood for enjoying anything. His relationship with Alex seemed to be over, and he was trying to convince himself that it was he who had ended it when he knew that it was she who had fallen out of love with him. He did not want to talk to anyone and was wondering how he was going to get home without any money. He would not ask anyone to lend him some. He imagined all of them turning him down or, if someone did, having to pay it back. He did not want to feel that he owed anyone anything. He remembered his bus pass. He cheered up slightly. He continued to ruminate about the group. He was fed up with all of them. He wasn't sure whether they really were all ganging up on him, but it certainly felt like it.

NINETEEN

❧

Today was a first on several counts. Seeing the group only in the gym or, at best, at an occasional birthday lunch they had formed an opinion of one another that they had begun to realize was one-dimensional. They had persisted in this opinion partly because some felt they had found what they had been looking for and did not want to make any changes to it but also because they all – apart from Silas – seemed to be happy playing the role that the others had imposed on them. This view was changing as they began to display sides to one another that had not previously been apparent.

Lola and Alex were lost in thoughtful wonderment as they wandered around Benedict's workplace looking at the equipment he used for his projects. It was clear that he had skills and a life-style they had not previously considered. They were particularly impressed with a model of a very large alabaster tomb chest to be used for wet towels for the pool he had designed at the club of which he had spoken.

He had made no impression on either of them at the gym. They had seen him merely as thoughtful but quiet and, if any-thing, a passive rather than an active member of the group. He had switched in their thinking and in their appraisal into someone managerial, creative and with a concealed prosperity that his life-time's work as a partner in a firm of church architects had provided but which they had not previously noted.

'He's been very low profile,' Alex whispered to Lola. 'He's quite fanciable. What d'you think?'

'Not my type. Probably more yours.'

They both wondered why they were now taking a view of Benedict that having known him only in the gym prevented either of them from seeing him as anything other than as a member of the family.

'It's a break-out phenomenon. We are in a new role,' Jerry was saying to the others. 'It's as if we have only just met. As if we're strangers.'

'What do you mean?' said Harold. 'I don't feel I'm in a new role or a stranger. I feel just the same as I did when we arrived.' He wanted to tell them that he wished he hadn't worn such tight pants that morning. He didn't know why he did it. Habit, he supposed. But he remained certain that he did not like having the one he owned and, much more certain, having one at all. He would have to go to the toilet and rearrange things, otherwise he wouldn't be able to enjoy his lunch. He felt more strongly than ever that although he may have looked like he was a contented member of the group he was really only one on sufferance. He thought 'suffer' was a good word to describe how he was feeling at that moment. He moved slightly nearer to Silas. He liked Silas, but he knew it was only while he was hiding his penis. If he unstrapped it, things would be different. He might talk to him later. People were not always what they seemed.

'We feel more ourselves,' Alex said, because she liked drink, food and people she knew in a sunny outdoor setting but also because she wanted to hear what Benedict thought about what Jerry had said.

Harold, still wrapped up in thoughts about parts of himself that he hated and his need to hide them from the rest of the world, did not want to talk to Alex about the role she thought he might be playing. He was not interested in role-play. It was too close to home. He wondered whether she had sensed something. He decided to fade into the background for a while. Accepting Drago's offer of another drink he sat down carefully on an upturned wooden packing case in a corner of the yard. Its weathered surface looked as if it had seen many comings and goings over the years.

Benedict had only just noticed Alex. Of course, he had seen her many times, but she had changed from being one of the boys whom he had more or less ignored, because he resented her being in the group in the first place, to being an attractive woman whom he could not take his eyes off. He found certain girls irresistible. Out of the blue Alex had slipped into that category. He didn't know how it had happened, but it had. He was torn between knowing how easy it was to fall for someone and the realization that, however exciting and life-changing it might be, there was often a downside.

He wondered what had happened to the girl he had met when he had gone on his rock-climbing holiday in Scotland. He had talked about her, or at least tried to, at Harold's birthday lunch. He had fallen in love with her, but as usual it had not lasted. He had left her within a week of telling everyone that he had never met anyone so amazing and that he wanted to live with her. At least he did not suffer the sorrow unique to the one abandoned. He thought of her. It can't be nice having someone turn their back on you. If anyone did that to me, he told himself, I'd feel like killing myself.

Benedict's ruminations about love and its discontents had, for a change, been internal. He had noticed that this had been happening more often lately. He put it down to being lonely. If there's no one to talk to, it can't be unreasonable to talk to oneself. He'd had a girlfriend once who had completely put him off by humming whenever there was a gap in the conversation. When he had managed to pluck up courage to complain about it she had said that it was understandable in someone who had been living on her own for as long as she had. He had told her that she was now with him and that the humming was intrusive. She was unable to give it up, and taking the view that something had already come between them he ended the relationship.

Perhaps that's why he had invited the group to lunch, a family lunch. Of course, he did not want to kill himself. He hated violence in all its forms. He wanted to be with people. He wanted to test their feelings for him. Instead he replied, 'I think we must prepare ourselves for our next battle.'

Alex did not feel quite brave enough to query his comment, although she would have loved to have done so.

Jerry had no such problems with speaking up, particularly when no one had addressed him. 'Who's done what to you? Who do you want to go to war with? Whoever it was seems to have made you very angry.'

'I'm not angry.'

'Well, you seem to be very interested in war and conflict. Look at all those black-and-white pictures you've got on the wall in your studio of London burning during the Battle of Britain. And didn't I see a print of *The Charge of the Light Brigade* or something like it somewhere? I think you are girding your loins.'

Only Harold seemed to be interested in what Jerry was talking about. He was about to ask for further elaboration on loin-girding when Jerry beat him to it by asking Benedict, 'What's your hobby?'

Not realizing that Jerry's question was an extension of his belief that he was angrier than he would admit to and that his hobby might provide a clue to it, Benedict was pleased that the conversation had turned to the one thing he enjoyed. He was dying to talk about it. 'I'll be back in a moment,' he said.

When he returned he was carrying a dagger and a war hammer. 'These are replicas of the weapons used by the Knights at the Battle of Crécy. I designed these myself.'

'Is that what you keep in your playroom?' Jerry looked pleased that Benedict was confirming what he had thought.

Benedict ignored the enquiry. 'I also have a longbow. It's made from a single piece of yew wood. Wait a moment.' He went back into the studio and returned with it. He told his bewildered guests that the staves were cut in winter when no sap was running between the inner heart wood and the outer sap wood and that the two ends were joined by a length of cord. 'It takes enormous strength to pull it.' He said, looking to see whether any one was interested in his weapon collection. He was pleased to see that they all were. 'The bow was made to measure. It's more or less the same height as I am.'

He passed it around. They tested its flexibility and were amazed by the force required to bend it, if only an inch or two. Alex was totally overawed. Benedict was not sure whether it was by the bow or by him.

An arrow appeared in his hand. They wondered how it got there. Aiming his fourteenth-century missile at a target fixed to a wall, which until then no one had noticed, he fired the arrow at it. It struck the target with an enormous but virtually silent thud. When the unexpectedness of its power and the excitement caused by it had worn off, everyone wanted to try their hand but Benedict firmly but quietly said, 'Sorry, folks. It could still kill someone.'

And just as quietly, but only to himself, Jerry replied, 'What did I tell you?'

Alex could not understand what was happening. When Benedict's arrow hit the target she became aware of a sensation in her chest. It was not a pain, nor was it frightening. It was exciting, and it made her catch her breath. In fact, it was surprisingly agreeable.

What she would have liked was for Benedict to repeat his action so that she might better understand why she felt as she did. She knew she could not have seen the arrow striking the target. It had all happened too quickly, but she thought she had.

She told herself that it must be the alcohol and the excitement, if only temporarily, of feeling as if one was in a war zone. Her system must been struggling to reconcile a longbow-versus-crossbow battle fought almost seven hundred years earlier in Normandy with a re-enactment in a builder's yard in a south-London suburb. Benedict's longbow had won. Had her crossbow let her down? Or had she deliberately stood in the line of fire?

It was the almost inaudible dull thump that silenced all of them, but it was her unexpected response to it that impressed itself on Alex. She thought that no one else could have experienced such an emotional reaction. It had made her gasp. She liked that word. Her breathing was still affected by it. She knew what it was she wanted. She wanted to be Benedict's target. She wanted to be pierced by his arrow. She felt instead that she was playing the role of a character in a romantic novel written by a lonely old lady reliving a never-forgotten experience permanently embedded in her psyche. Common sense told her to rid herself of it. It would always cause problems. After all, it was just recently that she'd had a problem with it involving Silas. Perhaps she should ask a psychiatrist if he could excise it as a surgeon might something malignant, but at the same time she knew that what she really wanted was not that but the replacement of it with another sensation, not just a better one but one that would come with a guarantee of happiness, not sorrow.

The imagery of arrows and hearts was such a cliché. She couldn't believe that an adult woman could even be thinking in such terms, never mind considering it as an explanation for how she was feeling. It was not Valentine's Day. She was in a yard surrounded by a group of people who had never grown up and never been satisfied in the first place and were happily re-experiencing primitive needs which could never be satisfied in any other place.

None of them seemed to know that that was what they were doing. Not even Jerry. She thought he was fairly perceptive. But even he was still trying to find answers to questions that no one had asked him. She knew nothing of his difficult relationship with his father but wondered whether he realized that the questions were his own.

Jerry often thought of the questions to which his father had invariably replied facetiously. He behaved as his father had whenever someone asked him something. The questioner was seldom satisfied with his reply. No one knew what he was talking about. He could just as well have said, as his father had, that Y is a crooked letter. It seemed to be enough for Jerry that his listeners smiled when he spoke. That was all he needed. That the Lord's face would shine upon him. He was not going to find the Lord in Benedict's workplace and neither would she.

Alex's father may not have been in heaven, but Jerry's was. Her father was at home permanently mourning her mother. Even Silas had gained very little from believing that she had used the same perfume as his mother when he was a child. Mother-and-child games had not done much for either of them, although on reflection she thought she had learned quite a lot from them – at least enough to know that they did not have to be repeatedly played out. Perhaps she and Silas had been concerned at least to start with that; despite the happiness that they occasionally achieved together they had ultimately failed to rearrange their pasts with one another. It was probably because they were both looking for the same thing. Their relationship had not worked for them. Neither was too distressed by its ending. Being loved by a mother had been denied to both of them. They had not found what they were looking for, and, even if they had succeeded, they might well have ended up competing with one another for it. It had been fun for a while playing bows and arrows with Silas, but she had quickly come to realize that no long-term benefit was likely to come from it. Silas, in his role as Cupid, had almost pierced her heart with his arrow, but she had recovered quickly. Her heart had not been broken, only damaged slightly. Going regularly to the gym was the treatment for heart problems. She did realize that in her case it was also the cause.

Could Cupid's arrow damage the heart physically as well as emotionally? It might be a coincidence that all the group members had heart problems, more of one sort than another perhaps, but no one could deny that most of them had probably been at risk if not for coronary artery disease then for affairs of the heart of one kind or another. She was about to say to Benedict that his bow should carry a health warning when he turned to her and smiled.

Was there a message to her in his smile? If there was she would have to decode it. She would interpret it later. She needed more information.

'I'm sorry if I startled you,' he said. He looked at her but said nothing more.

She felt penetrated by his look and found herself thinking: not again – and a moment later asking herself why that was what she was thinking. Had he heard her silent wish? Aware that his eyes were green, something she had not previously noticed, stopped her from making a joke out of something that could so easily be misinterpreted. If she wanted to continue thinking in metaphors she might have said that his arrow could be charged with unwanted penetration. But it was not unwanted, and she welcomed it. She was not his target, but she would like to play the role of willing victim. Sex with Benedict was not going to happen because he seemed totally unaware of the effect his demonstration of overwhelming power, as applied to the wars of time past, had on her. No wonder breaking and entering, the invasion of another's space, the rape of an enemy's women was as often a feature of warfare as it was of crime. Power must be the most potent aphrodisiac of all. She recalled from her school days that *puissance* translated as sexual potency as well as power.

The imaginary striking of a gong, the call to eat and Benedict's seating instructions were followed by the serving of the first course. Was it only she who was going to have to wait for satisfaction of her appetite, only she who wanted to believe it was all a coded message from Benedict and directed uniquely at her? Did any of the others realize how much the symbolism of it all might be contributing to their enjoyment as much as it did hers?

She sat next to the baffling Jerry, while Benedict served them out of the frying pan on to the plates in front of them.

'Better than into the fire.' Those who were still tuned into the here and now rather than into the there and then heard Jerry's comment and smiled. And as the self-appointed court jester his ego became ever more highly polished until he imagined he could see his face reflected in it.

Alex wished she could send a message to Benedict that only he would understand. She tried out a few food-related ones in her mind. 'Warms the cockles of the heart,' she thought might work, although she was not too sure what cockles were. Perhaps it applied more to drink than food. Drago, who was now in charge of wine, might know what she meant. Benedict would not. Looking at Benedict she settled for 'Fantastic starter!', but immediately changed her mind to what she thought was the more intimate 'We're off to a good start' followed by 'I love fried potatoes.'

She was brought down to earth by his reply. 'First of the Jersey Royals. I was lucky to find them.'

Harold – who until then had been rather quiet but who was feeling more comfortable having sorted out his problem – now tuned into a conversation that for at least one of them was going nowhere. He reminded them of the time when there had been a potato famine in Ireland.

Silas, who sensed that Alex was flirting with Benedict, had come to see all relationships as a game of chess where someone has to lose. Since it was usually him, he wanted to block her next move as retaliation for her having turned her back on him. He would have liked to have said 'Checkmate', but she was no longer his mate and never likely to be.

'Potatoes were common currency in Ireland during the Famine,' said Benedict 'The economy had crashed, and those who could went to America or landed up here. We're running out of potatoes here now, well, money anyway. We're stuck. We should be going to Ireland, since history usually repeats itself.'

Lola said, 'My mother's Irish.' Her comment turned out to be a conversation-blocker, and for the moment any further discussion of the economy, Irish or otherwise, came to a halt.

Time passed not with pleasantries such as 'Pass the salt' (since there wasn't any) but with eating and murmurs of appreciation until Jerry said, 'My grandfather didn't want to fight in the Great War, although he was eventually called up and he had to. He wanted to run away to Ireland. He told everyone he was enlisting in the Royal Irish Runners. There were quite a few people at the time wanting to join the RIR.'

They agreed that the First World War was a catastrophe that should never have happened.

Harold, who thought of himself as a monarchist since he had discovered that he and Prince Philip shared the same birthday, spoke of his hero King George V. 'He phoned him up, you know.' The others waited to hear who it was that the King had telephoned. 'They were upset with one another because both thought that their granny Hanover preferred the other one.'

Drago was trying to remember how often he had filled Harold's glass. He remembered that he'd had three Bellinis before lunch.

Harold's voice was definitely slurry. 'George thought he could sort it out on the phone. He rang Cousin Wilhelm once or twice,' – he had been about to say Cousin Willy but thought better of it – 'but the Kaiser had his reputation to keep up. He would have none of it. I expect he told George that the time to have put things right was when they were children. Their nannies could have dealt with it then. Even when they were adults they envied one another's toys. I think it was Wilhelm who had a really smart racing yacht. Or it might have been his father. Anyway the one with the smaller one was very jealous of the one with the bigger one,' quickly adding, 'Nothing wrong with having a yacht or a nanny.'

Jerry wondered why Harold was going on about nannies. They had spoken about nannies once before. He thought it was at the gym one morning. Jerry was not unaware that Harold was probably talking about the first war, not about nannies, but his past had not been a happy time, and he did not want to talk about nannies, whether his own or anyone else's.

Alex, who seldom spoke because, despite her acceptance by the group, she still thought she was there under false pretences, said, 'Trying to avoid violent solutions can't be condemned. George must have thought a friendly chat had to be better than a fight. Make love not war.'

She managed to catch Benedict's eye for a moment. He wondered why she was banging on about an overused and definitely out-of-date anti-Vietnam War slogan. He thought after a few moments that she might be talking to him. How many arrows can one bowman keep in his quiver? he asked himself. Perhaps she was right. He was beginning to be bored with his preoccupation with the past, particularly past battles. Crécy had been over in a few hours. Love, if handled properly, could last much longer.

TWENTY

❧

Lunch finally lurched into empty-plate territory. The warmth of the day, the effects of the wine and perhaps the presence of the two women, now an accepted feature of the men's group, had left them relaxed and ready to depart. Drago, doing what was second nature for him, although no one else including their host noticed, had stacked the plates and was looking for the sink. Alex and Lola had said goodbye and thanked Benedict for what had turned out for both of them to be a rewarding extension of their gym encounters, and Corker had also left without for once making it seem as if he was taking a curtain call.

'Stage two seemed to go off well.' Benedict's comment was received with the usual indifference and even a few nods of agreement.

Only Jerry's puzzled expression showed that he was interested in what Benedict had said. He had always thought of himself as the group's leader, although he knew that it neither had one nor needed one. The ethos of the group was that it acted as a single unit when decision-making, or what passed for decision-making, was required, mainly because there were seldom decisions to be made. Shall we go to Franco's for lunch or to Dino's could hardly be a cause for contentious discussion. The answer was always a 'Don't mind' or a pause while waiting for someone else to decide. What stopped Jerry in his tracks was that Benedict had caught him unawares. He had introduced a new topic. It was not something that he or the others were being asked to give a view on. It was a bald statement of fact.

What did Benedict mean? Stage two had gone off well. It suggested to Jerry that there must be a stage three in the offing on which he had not been briefed and also a stage one which seemed to have come and gone without anyone remarking on its passing. He was preparing to be offended. It was an issue that should first have been put to the committee. He reminded himself that there was no committee and never likely to be one, and even if there were one no one would ever have put anything to it. Jerry none the less thought of himself as its chairman. He was offended because he had not been asked to give his seal of approval. No one had even discussed it with him. A decision had been made or was about to be made behind his back. That was enough to hurt anyone's feelings.

Benedict, fresh from playing fourteenth-century war games with Alex, was in a light-hearted and perceptive mood. Reaching out his hand to Jerry and resting it on the sleeve of his jacket he enquired, 'What's up?'

There was nothing that Jerry disliked more than having a man touch him, except maybe a man asking him what the matter was. He felt patronized. It reminded him of his father's inability to treat him as a human being. He was the one who since childhood had asked irritating questions. It was he who had been brought up to feel fobbed off, not Benedict. His main reason for joining the police was because he knew that ultimately, if he played his cards right, the time would come when he would make the decisions and not have to answer to anyone. A resolution, an important one by the sound of it and about which he might have been kept deliberately in the dark, seemed about to be taken out of his hands.

Jerry knew that he had certain foibles. He had often been told by well-meaning friends that he was hypersensitive and took offence too easily, and he also knew that everyone referred to him as a control freak behind his back. They were probably right. As a child, from the nursery onwards, he had never been able to trust any of his controllers. It was not surprising that if any controlling needed to be done he would insist upon doing it himself. He thought back to when he had retired from the police and had decided to train as a psychotherapist. There were many courses available, and in the course of time he had obtained a master's degree in family therapy. It was no mean feat at his age, and those who knew him well had shared his pride in the achievement. He had no intention of practising as a therapist. He only wanted one client and that was himself. An increase in self-knowledge had helped enormously. Attending the gym and making new friends had made him realize that there were people who were interested in what he had to say. His father might well have been interested in him but had never made it at all clear. His friends in the group listened to one another. No one talked over anyone or replied mockingly. He had been brought up to believe that a mocking reply was acceptable. It had taken him a lifetime to discover that it was not. Even his mother was probably a victim of his father's witticisms. He remembered one of her favourite comments. She would frequently remind him that sarcasm was the lowest form of wit.

He had never mentioned to the others that he was a therapist. Not because he was ashamed of it. It was more to do with the fact that he was his only client. He felt it a weakness that he needed help with emotional problems, despite his training. He had never thought of it as a weakness in others if they decided to discuss their issues with someone, but he certainly thought it was a flaw in his character when he did. He had always worn his 'I don't need anybody' face when he was in the police force. He had been brought

148

up to value self-sufficiency by his carers far too early in life. He remembered being told what a clever boy he was when he was four because he could do up his shoelaces. He had tried to convince himself that he could get by better with not needing others. How wrong that had been. All that had done was to condemn him to a lifetime of loneliness.

Everyone looked for strong leadership, and he believed that he had been able to convince his work colleagues that he could provide it. Being in the force had brought to the fore virtues such as obedience, seeing things in black and white, stark do's and don'ts – but mainly don'ts. Being in the group had changed things. He had come to see that leadership in the world that he had left behind might have been an asset, but it was no longer an asset in the world in which he now lived. It could even be a liability. People might depend on you to do things for them. He did not want to attract misfits like himself who were unable to do things for themselves. Had he been a misfit? Could he have been the dependent one he was thinking of? The answer to that was a reluctant yes.

He thought of the others. None of them were like him. They were all talented and successful. He didn't think that any of them thought they were misfits. If one did, he had got over it during his working life just as he had tried to do. He realized that the group, because it was so accepting and non-demanding, allowed all of them to value being rather than doing. Doing must have been an essential feature of their lives before their heart problems and, he thought, in some cases might even have contributed to them.

Jerry was pleased that he had managed to work that one out. It helped him understand why no one minded how odd or strange any of the others were. They were happy to be themselves while they were together. There was no one to sit in judgement over them, no one whose benevolence was essential to their well-being and no one to whom they had to kowtow because he was paying their wages. That was why they had got on together in the first place when they were all dressed like clones. Lucky they had come to like one another as people, otherwise their finding out about one another, as in their lunch party, which on this occasion revealed Benedict as he was rather than how the others believed him to be, might possibly have led to the breaking up of the group. He wondered whether they would be able to withstand their loss of anonymity. Would knowing who they were or even why they were become a problem, since not knowing had clearly been an asset? Would friendship withstand the absence of illusion?

Jerry also realized that leadership, an issue to which he had given much credence in the past, was not something necessarily acquired by appointment or promotion or by passing an examination. It was something else, something difficult to put one's finger on. It was an asset, like intuition. Some had it, and others did not. It was with a shock that he realized that he probably did not have it and that Benedict did. When Benedict had said that stage two had gone off well, what he may have meant was that not only was stage three about to begin but the process of knowing who they really were rather than how they represented themselves in the real world had also begun.

TWENTY-ONE

When Silas arrived at the gym the following week the group were talking about a discussion on networking that Harold had heard the tail end of on the radio that morning. Tweeting and texting and other forms of electronic communication had been considered a good thing by a public-relations guru for those wanting immediacy of contact with those needed to fulfil the promotional needs of their clients but to a lesser extent for remaining in touch with their friends. The guru had said that there was nothing to beat face-to-face interaction not only at work but as an exercise for the mind. As the interviewer had put it, 'It was like going to the gym was for the body.' Everyone was heartened by this exchange of views, seeing it as confirmation that what they were doing met with an expert's approval. They were pleased with themselves for being ahead of or at least abreast of the times.

What seemed strange to Silas was that there was no mention of the previous week's lunch at Benedict's place. The party had come and gone, and it was as if it had never been. No one alluded to it. Should anyone have wanted to exercise his freedom of expression, a freedom that was a *sine qua non* and never questioned and criticize any aspect of it, they all knew that it would have run no risk of offending Benedict. Although he was exercising in the conference room and would have known nothing of their discussion, adverse comments would not concern him.

Silas imagined him saying, 'I did my best, and if they didn't enjoy it I'm sorry to hear it.' He thought he would have probably added, probably under his breath because he was polite and would not want to hurt anyone's feelings, something to the effect that 'I'm not responsible for how others feel, and there's nothing I can do about it anyway.'

Silas knew that if anyone had not enjoyed something he had arranged it would immediately have become a problem. He would have been upset about it for weeks. What seemed so extraordinary was that no one had made any comment of any kind, whether of criticism or praise, of an event that at the very least was an unusual one. How many people would have been capable of cooking and serving a meal, preceded by champagne cocktails (or the Italian equivalent), in a builder's yard as elegantly as Benedict? He wanted someone to bring the subject up because he had planned to use the lunch as a hook on which to hang an announcement that he had been winding himself up to make for the past few weeks. It was not that the party had not been successful – because it had. If anything it had been too successful because it had brought into focus how he felt about himself and about what he wanted to tell the group. If there was a downside it was because it had reminded him of life events to which he would usually shut his eyes; a reminder, for him at least, of what was not rather than what was. Did he also resent that they had never mentioned it afterwards despite everyone thinking it was great at the time? That annoyed him because they took into their stride a *laissez-faire* attitude to what life was about. It was not what it was about. Not for him. What was missing was gratitude. That was what distressed him. Without gratitude nothing is valued. God had provided, but that did not prevent them from thanking him for so doing.

He wondered whether they were waiting for someone to bring up the lunch topic, just as they had stood on the doorstep of Benedict's studio a week earlier waiting for someone to ring the doorbell. Were they all suffering from an 'After you' complex? He cheered up slightly. Had he just invented a new disorder? Yes, that's what's wrong with them. They are all too polite. That was one way of looking at it, but he had not given up on the feeling that he had been patronized. He wished he could as easily put his finger on a complex like that in his own life. He would love to know what was wrong with him. He knew he was not happy. He had probably never been happy. He was too sensitive to how he believed others thought about him. He was offended easily when it was obvious that no offence was intended, and he would dwell on an imagined 'wrong' that had been done to him for a considerable time. He realized that having a father and a mother with no time for him must have had a lot to do with it, but he didn't know how to deal with how it made him feel. Trying to make changes within himself might be easier and certainly more sensible than trying to persuade everyone else in his social circle to change, but he had no idea of how to go about it.

What had really been troubling him for some time was that his life was in such a mess. He found himself unable to discuss it with any of the others or even admit that he had problems with which he was unable to cope. It had come to a head last week because he had resented everyone enjoying themselves at the lunch when he obviously had not.

Drago was also puzzled by the group's failure to acknowledge an event in which he felt he had played a significant role in helping it to go off as well as it had. He did not join in the discussion that had now moved on from networking to whether it was wise to permit young Amish people who had had a God-fearing and strictly moral upbringing in the backwoods of Philadelphia to spend a year exposed to the wickedness of life in the outside world, because he was lost in his own thoughts. He was not

153

brooding. The war years had taught him that. Looking back in anger had prevented so many of his friends from moving on. After a few minutes of reflection it came to him that however much the group may have enjoyed Benedict's 'outside world' experiment the previous week they felt more at home in the abstractions of the gym world than in the realities of the real one. We are like the Amish, he thought. We have faith in our way of thinking and our way of doing things. We do not want a disorderly life of drinking, drugs and dirty dancing. He smiled. He liked the alliteration. His English was improving all the time. It was a self-congratulatory smile. Going out with that English girl all those years ago, who had been sent for work experience by a travel agency to what was then Yugoslavia, must have done him some good after all.

Jerry was not particularly surprised that no one discussed the lunch. He was more surprised by how much he had enjoyed not only the food but everything else there. *Lunch in the Builder's Yard.* He liked calling it that. It rolled off the tongue, like the title of a book he might one day write. He wondered whether there was enough poetry left in him for a book after his father's repeated put-downs while he was growing up. It might not fill a book, but it should be enough for a short story.

He had thought the lunch party magical. It appealed to him on many levels. Whether it was the extraordinary brightness of the light reflected from the corrugated metal roof of Benedict's work-place shining down upon them, or the sparkling conversation, or the savour of the food, or the effect of the alcohol, or their changing perception of one another when they were no longer in their familiar setting, or because they were in holiday mode, he did not know.

What he did know was that it had allowed him to see his friends in a different light. There was more to them that he had been aware of. He wondered about Benedict. His quiet and thoughtful persona had an angry, possibly violent, side to it that he had not noticed hitherto. There was the arrow aimed at the very heart of things and Alex's heavily disguised but obviously very interested reaction to the symbolism of it; there were the war pictures displayed on Benedict's wall, the *Charge of the Light Brigade* that he was still saddened by after more than 150 years, the sepia photographs of the trenches in the First World War.

He thought of Drago's comments at variance with the upbringing he had hinted at but seemed not to want to share with them. There was the fading into the background of Silas and the contribution that he might have made but had chosen not to. Even the group's departure in contrast to its arrival had a significance on which Jerry could not help reflecting. The harmony of the lunch had been the link that had connected the jumbled and hesitant disorder of their coming with the slow drifting departure of their going. The guests left in a sequence that balanced their need to return to the real world against their wish to remain for a little longer in the world of their imagination. Only Silas returned home on his own. Only Silas left early. It was only Silas whose departure was marked.

A week later Jerry noted as he listened to the others that life for them went on as before. The group, its reason for being, its discussions, its outlook on the world and its unspoken influences on each other, continued as ever to exercise their thinking. If anyone had thought that the lunch had been a revelation, a herald of something entirely new, they kept it to themselves or were waiting for someone to tell them what it was.

Silas was also waiting, not particularly patiently, for an opening in the conversation so that he could make what he thought of as his momentous announcement. He failed to find one. If anyone noticed that he was looking anxious they did not comment. Silas had prepared himself for a debate, the agenda of which was burning a hole in his thinking. But there was no such debate.

They had got no closer to discussing it than Luc telling them that a new restaurant had opened next to the gym. They looked at him, waiting for him to open up a discussion. Discussions concerning food and its preparation were always of interest. Appreciation of the effort made by a provider apparently was not.

Silas seized his chance. 'What did you think of the lunch last week?'

The others were still thinking about the new restaurant. They might try it next time it was someone's birthday. They considered Silas's question. Had any of them sensed a note of discord in his voice? There was a murmur of appreciation from one or two of them and a nod of approval from Luc as they stood up and wandered off, perhaps rather more quickly than usual, to their exercise class.

TWENTY-TWO

Silas was left reflecting on what he had wanted to share with the others and irritated that he had let an opportunity to do so slip by. He had planned to tell them that he thought the group was drifting in a direction with which he was not happy; also that there was too great a contrast between a lifestyle to which they all seemed to subscribe and with which everyone appeared happy and how he felt about life, particular his own. The lunch had been the last straw. There had been a bonhomie in the air with more than a hint of silver-spoon contentment set against a background which he had convinced himself that not only did he not envy but which, more than that, he actively resented. They had come across as too happy. They had acted as if life was for ever dealing them good cards, and, worse, they were presenting an image of themselves that suggested to anyone who had previously never met them that they hadn't a care in the world. It could not be true. It was certainly not like that for him, and he didn't like the body language of the group informing him that it was like that for them. The champagne cocktail, or whatever it was Drago called it, and the archery demonstration, never mind arriving in two taxis, was over the top. He blamed Benedict's lunch, and he blamed Benedict for having the idea of an alfresco lunch in the first place, and he blamed the weather for providing the perfect setting.

He preferred the group as it was in the beginning, before

they celebrated birthdays and went to one another's homes, when they accepted each other just as they were – elderly males with heart problems who had been recommended regular supervised exercise. What he could not cope with was not just their enjoyment of life or at least making the best of it but their insistence on demonstrating their enjoyment. He had deliberately not turned up for Harold's birthday celebration and had hoped that they would get the message then. No one had asked him to explain his absence when next they had met. That annoyed him. Getting to know one another had been a mistake. He did not want revelation; he wanted concealment. It did not occur to him that the group accepted one another exactly as they were. Social or other distinctions had never been on the agenda. He was surprised that it had become so for him. He could see that the gym gave one the opportunity to make new friends and discuss personal lives. It was an agreeable way of passing an hour or so. But it had become too personal. The few friends he had made had become a clique, a private members' club of which he did not want to be a member. They had childish rules. It was all too ridiculous. He blamed Benedict. He was a practical joker whom everyone took seriously. He did not even take himself seriously. Jerry encouraged him, and the others went along with it. It was definitely not for him. A thought went through his mind. What would it take for it to be for him? What would allow him to enjoy it? He knew the answer but did not want to acknowledge it, even to himself. He wanted to be in charge. He wanted to make the rules. He wanted to decide where or whether to go for lunch. Above all, he did not believe in contentment after meals.

Perhaps they did it to irritate him. Well, maybe not, but he did have something to hide from them. He did not know whether that was the real reason for the way he was feeling. He had not been open with them. He felt a familiar self-reproach coming on. His entire life was a lie. He had not even been honest with himself. It was hard for him to tell them what was actually going on in his life, because it was too complicated, and anyway he was ashamed of it.

His life had always been a mess, but it had taken a turn for the worse since he and Alex decided to call it a day. He had thought he had found what he was looking for in her. But it was not long before he realized that their relationship was no different from every one of the others that had gone before. It was just more of the same. She was no more interested in him than anyone else had been. He should have learned by now that falling in love with 'mothers', actual or surrogate, would be a waste of time.

He had to talk to someone about it. His idea of telling the group was probably not a good one. They would be as embarrassed as he would likely be. Anyway they were seldom all together at the same time, and he did not want an account of the discussion passed on to the absentees with casual variations added because they had forgotten what he had actually said. Chinese whispers; not a good idea. He felt relieved. He liked putting things off. It was second nature. He would ring one of them and take him out for a drink. But who should he choose? He thought of Jerry and realized he would be too likely to reinterpret and misinterpret what he was telling him, and he did not want that. He could not tune into Drago. Luc was too maternal. Harold? He hardly knew Harold. He was an unsolved jigsaw puzzle with too many pieces missing. Corker might be helpful, but he did not have his telephone number. He could not even look it up because he didn't know his surname. Was Corker his surname or his stage name?

He would call Benedict, although he was angry with him. He would get over it. He was as much an unknown quantity as he was, although rather less of an unknown quantity since the lunch. It was true that much had been revealed, but there had to be a lot more going on than he had let on. He had not even told anyone he was a church architect; a well-known one apparently to go by the glimpses he'd had of some of the drawings in his studio. Silas had not realized that Benedict took life so seriously. His gym persona was very different. He had thought of him as easy-going and friendly, but he had not even smiled when Jerry had asked him – when the two women were not around – whether a well-known erection in the area had been his. The others were moderately amused, but he was not. Instead he had said something cryptic like achievement, potency and tower blocks usually go hand in hand and then smiled but only to himself. Silas thought he knew what he was getting at but couldn't be sure. The new Benedict was a bit of an enigma, but the old one had seemed keen on anonymity. He decided that on balance Benedict would be his confidant. He phoned him immediately before he changed his mind about doing so and arranged to meet him in the in the park café the following morning.

Silas arrived first and waited nervously. Perhaps Benedict had decided not to come. He would feel terrible if he didn't turn up without letting him know. He wouldn't be able to cope with that. It would be a real snub. His self-defeating reverie was disturbed by the other's arrival. He was less than five minutes late, but it took Silas a few minutes before he could shake off his negative feelings. These had become more frequent lately. He wondered who he could blame for how he felt. It could be Alex. It could be any of the others. It was probably all of them.

Benedict seemed different. He seemed apprehensive. About what Silas had no idea. He had built him up in his mind as a rock to lean on, a fount of wisdom into whom he could tap and a buddy on whom he would be able to rely. He had been looking forward to talking to him, despite his reservations about extra-curricular meetings. He was having second thoughts.

Benedict was wondering why he had been summoned. He felt as he often had at school. He was in the headmaster's study about to be admonished for something he had done and with which he hoped he had got away but which he obviously had not. He was also irritated because he was in the middle of a project with a deadline approaching, and Silas was a minimally active sculptor and could take time off whenever he felt like it.

He thought he knew what Silas wanted to talk about. He must have found out about Alex and was angry with him for trying to steal his girlfriend. How that could have come about he couldn't imagine. No one could have told him because no one had known about it. Neither did he or Alex, although either of them might have hoped that something might have evolved from that magical moment when he was showing off his archery. Nothing of substance had. Maybe Silas had sensed something. He would have to be careful. The man had a temper. He didn't want him to lash out suddenly and break his glasses. What made him think about his glasses? Was he beginning to see things more clearly?

The café was beginning to fill up with tourists. Each waited for the other to speak. Silas wondered how to bring up what was on his mind, but the idea of Benedict as his confessor was rapidly becoming less attractive. It was his manner. Silas did not know how to interpret it. Benedict seemed different. He was easier to talk to in the gym. It was only a week, but he had changed and was clearly not waiting with bated breath to hear what Silas had to say. Both were uncomfortable.

Benedict was preoccupied with an earlier waiting that had nothing to do with Silas. He was waiting for the blow to fall, the reprimand to find its target, the excuses and explanations he would be called upon to make, the misdeeds – not that there were any – for which he would be called to account.

But Silas was not in the least intuitive. Had he been, his life might have been different. He had been provided with minimal input as a child, and like other loveless children he was more comfortable with those who had suffered in the same way. But he had never tried to understand anyone else's suffering. He had made no effort to help anyone or even empathize. He had instead seen others like he saw everyone as failed providers whom he believed promised everything but who delivered nothing. The loveless might once have been his friends but soon became his rivals. They competed with him for the attention of an imaginary rescue service, which never arrived but for which they all impatiently waited.

Everyone in the group seemed to have been more successful than he in coping with life. Silas resented their success. He blamed them for their interactions with one another, for highlighting and drawing his attention to his misfortunes. He had been happier when he knew nothing about them and when they knew nothing about him. He could not envy anything about which he knew nothing. He blamed Benedict for rescuing them from anonymity and for illuminating all of them with a light brighter than they deserved. He preferred to remain in the shadows. It was too late for that now. Revelation might be fine for some but only for those who had nothing to hide.

Benedict, too, was in a negative mood. He was preparing himself for failure. He had convinced himself that his whole life had been a failure. He could remember as if it were yesterday his father telling him that he was no good. A loser, he had called him. 'You'll never be any good' was a phrase that was always some-where in his thinking. He was never entirely rid of it. There were distractions. Sex was one of them. He found it difficult sometimes to remember how his father looked, but he never forgot how he spoke, never forgot that he had referred to him as a loser.

That word – he could not even bring himself to even think of it – also echoed in his head whenever he took on a new project. It was hardly surprising that he set up situations in which failure was inevitable. He was good at self-fulfilling prophesies. He could see clearly why he was happy in the group. None of them expected anything of anyone. They were all equals. No one was more equal than anyone else. Had he spoiled everything by suggesting that they came to where he worked, suggesting that he cook for them – when it had all been Luc's idea in the first place? Had he been the cause of his own downfall? Perhaps it would have been better to have left well alone.

Jerry had been wrong when he called the lunch party a break-out phenomenon. What was surprising was that despite the hot-house atmosphere of their meetings that had begun in the gym, but now continued wherever they happened to be, they remained as close and as committed to one another as ever they had been. Where they were was never in conflict with why they were. Jerry was wrong about describing being elsewhere as a break-out phenomenon. He was wrong because they existed as a group. Their discussions may have reminded them of earlier life events that continued to influence them, but no one commented on them. Being together generated a non-verbal interaction that had brought to the surface thoughts and feelings that years of psychotherapy might have failed to elicit. Where they were was not important. The lunch had changed nothing. Their commitment remained as strong as ever. The location did not affect how they felt. It was enough that there had been a fleeting reminder, another look at their feelings, enough to realize that no one now needed to be scapegoated for whatever had gone wrong in the past. None of them was condemnatory, as his father had been.

It was only Silas who insisted on playing out his outsider role. Meeting him one to one was a mistake. He was committed only to sabotage. It was bringing back all the old feelings. Had he given up the idea of acceptance too soon, before he had learned not to return repeatedly to square one?

Benedict knew he was sometimes in the Crimea at the foot of the hill on a battlefield the world had never forgotten. He was Lord Cardigan passing on ill-thought-out orders to his commanders in the field. He was his father giving him faulty advice. He must not continue making the same mistakes. He would not be forgiven a second time. He had lost the entire Light Brigade. The 600 had died needlessly because of his father. From where would the attack come this time? From which quarter should he expect it? He shivered. It would be another uphill struggle. Silas had now become the enemy. The battle was never ending.

When Jerry told him at the party that he thought that there was conflict in his life he had denied it. But Jerry was right. There were historic battles in which he took an interest and he did like archery, but what concerned him most was not so much fighting but the enormity of loss. He had not realized that his interests and his work and his relationships were all battles he had to win. He realized with a shock that every battle that really fascinated him had already been lost. His print of Guernica on the wall in front of his desk was there not because it demonstrated the destructive power of German dive bombers but because it was a reminder of the violence inflicted upon the helpless. It was their deaths, their failure to survive, that Picasso had painted. The photographs of the Blitz, the 40,000 Londoners killed in the air raids, the Battle of the Somme in which Lord Haig sent 58,000 men and boys to their deaths on one day in July, the 600 dead in the Crimea, the 30,000 dead Frenchmen at Crécy were illustrations not of conflict but of bereavement. They were Benedict's memorials. His memories of losers. He had to climb out of the valley of death before loss overwhelmed him.

He wished he hadn't come. He looked at Silas and saw someone he no longer liked. He was not an enemy, like the Russians at Balaclava or the French at Crécy, but he was not exactly a friend. Had Silas become an obstacle in his path? He had not gone to the gym to be confronted with conflict. What he had found there was peace, tolerance and acceptance. He was opposed to warfare. He hated it. He was only interested in it as a historical concept, as a message from the past on how to avoid conflict in the present. The last thing he wanted was to perpetuate it. He was pleasantly surprised to find that the gym had smoothed the road down which he had been drifting. He was not sure how it had done that, but it had. He liked it that way. He wanted to go home and get on with his work, not take the morning off to discuss violence with Silas. He realized that he did not like confrontation. It made him uncomfortable. He had enjoyed last week because he felt that he was the conductor of the orchestra with all the players doing what was expected of them. Harmony had been the keynote of the builder's yard lunch. Silas was no longer singing from the same hymn sheet. He was a discordant element.

'I've just remembered something,' he said. 'You'll have to excuse me. I've got to dash. See you next week.'

Silas bought himself an espresso. He needed one. He might have a chocolate brownie not because he was unhappy or angry or needed to be comforted but because he was relieved and felt that he had something to celebrate. There was no one who he would want to talk to about his problems. No one in the group could help him. At the first hint of conflict or disharmony their camaraderie would cease. They would return to being strangers who might encounter one another in a supermarket or on a bus. He brightened up as he thought of such an outcome. He would like that. He did not have built-in harmony and he did not feel comfortable with those who did.

He must have been desperate. He knew now why internet dating attracted him. It was absolutely anonymous and impersonal. He liked that. Both parties were always guarded, frightened to give their names, hiding their true selves. If they had something to hide the internet was not the place for them. He had treated the group as he had the internet. When he found out the truth he did not like it. Already he was negotiating a divorce. He should never have used the internet to meet someone because he was not being genuine with them. It may have been his social life. It may have comforted him because it allowed him to meet women who might in some way, he never quite knew how, make up to him for the unhappy time he had had as a child. The fact that it had never worked did not put him off trying. It could never work for him, and neither could the group. The concept of genuine relationships was foreign to his experience.

He had never spent more than two weeks with anyone he had met through the internet except once. He had been immediately attracted to Maggie. He had seen something in her that was so attractive that he couldn't resist wanting to get to know her better. She was so much like him. She had lied to him as he had to her. She had not told him about her own abusive upbringing and its outcome, and neither had he told her about his. But when she did he felt even closer to her. She had represented herself as young, unmarried, free and available. Some of it was true. It was several months before he discovered that she was a mother with an eight-year-old son who was in the care of the local authority because when life became too impossible she would hit him. He remembered feeling not angry that she had deceived him but strangely pleased that a mother with a young son was taking such an interest in him. If their relationship had been in the past and was now over that might have been one thing. But it was not in the past. It was very much in the occasional present. They were drawn together for brief periods to re-enact their abusive pasts with one another.

He did not want to see Alex any more because he knew that what they had may have been gratifying for a while but it had meant no more than many other similar encounters. Although she had given him up, a situation with which he was never comfortable, he was able to recognize that if it had been up to him he would have continued to see her only until his next victim appeared on the horizon. He wanted to tell the group that he did not want to see any of them any more. He did not want to be reminded of their successes, nor did he want them to act as his conscience. They were too judgemental. They had taken a view about him. They talked about him behind his back. It would be nothing favourable. He no longer trusted them. Something was telling him that he had given up too soon. But something also told him that all would have been well had he not got to know them as they actually were, rather than as he wanted them to be. He had been given an opportunity to think about his life by the twice-weekly coming together of a group that by chance had turned into a therapeutic intervention that might continue for them but which he believed was too late for him. As he walked towards the tube station he reflected on his need to hide his inner self from the others. He knew that he had not been straightforward, possibly with any of them. It could be argued that it was not their concern. But he certainly had not been open with Alex. What he was going to discuss with Benedict would not only have shocked him but would probably have ended their relationship. When he thought about it he wondered how he could have behaved so badly. He also wondered why the group he was once so pleased to have been a part of now seemed to wish to exclude him.

TWENTY-THREE

Silas went home and phoned Luc. 'I've decided not to come to the gym any more. I might come in occasionally but probably on a day when the others aren't there.'

That was rather abrupt. He had not even said hello. Was he trying to shock Luc? Why would he want to do that? He knew why. It was because he wanted to hear him say how disappointed he was. He wanted to hear him try to persuade him to change his mind. He waited for him to say, 'Don't do that! We'll miss you. The others will be really upset.' But Luc did not. He did not know what to say. He thought he should tell Silas that he was making a mistake, but wishing not to sound too paternalistic decided to say nothing. Neither did he say that he should come to the gym and tell everyone. They could all have discussed it. He knew that it was no one's business if Silas had decided to give up, and he was sure that he must have a good reason for wanting to do so, but at the same time they were all very close and there were some things that they owed one another, and explanations of departure was one of them. It was too sudden. If he had not said anything, nor made such an issue of it and just drifted off, by the time anyone had noticed he had gone he would have faded from memory. There had been someone like that last year. He thought his name was Ed. He had come for the Christmas lunch and had not been seen since. In fact it was Silas who after a month or two had called him. Ed had told him that he had a lot on right then and would try to come before long, but he had never turned up. No one was in the least bothered by that. It had turned out that Ed was ill, and some months later they had heard he had died. Of course that was sad, and if they had known about it they would have sent a card to his wife. But that was different. Ed was someone they passed the time of day with. It was long before the group had evolved into what it was now.

It was also different with Silas. It was not only that he was part of the group but they had been together for a long time and had got on well with one another. Luc suddenly realized that leaving the group must have some significance, probably not too dissimilar to remaining in it. He couldn't think what it might be. But it must be important. Silas might be as much in the dark about it as he was. He reassured himself that Benedict or Jerry would know what it was, and, even if they didn't, it wouldn't prevent them from offering an explanation that would satisfy everyone. He couldn't wait to tell them next week.

He said, 'Sorry about that, Silas.' That did not seem to be much of a response to what the man obviously thought of as a startling announcement, but he couldn't think of anything more sensible to say. He hoped that the other might provide him with more information, something that he could get his teeth into at least. Even though he knew that Silas was suffering he could not help thinking how funny it was that food was something that never failed to come to his mind.

But he really was worried about Silas. Things were not going well for him. Everyone knew that he had been unhappy about something for some time, but he had not said what it was. No one had seen much of him for about three weeks. He hadn't come to Harold's birthday, but he had come to Benedict's lunch, although he hadn't looked as if he was enjoying it. He wasn't too sure whether there actually was a problem. He had assumed that if there was one it must be something that he did not want to talk about, and neither he nor anyone else had thought to be in touch with him about it away from the group.

Silas felt that he had to say something more to Luc. After all, he had called him. He could not just leave it like that. On the other hand, it would not be any good going through all the many resentments that had built up within him about everyone becoming too involved with one another when they were not at the gym. As he thought about it, it did seem a bit feeble.

Instead he said, 'I think that Benedict has become very pretentious lately. I know that he made a big effort over the lunch at his place, but it was too over the top. Going to the gym is one thing. It's nice occasionally to have a bit of a chat afterwards for a few minutes, but we seem to have turned ourselves into some sort of team with rules and obligations, and I don't like it. I just want to come to the gym, do the work-out and go home afterwards.'

He knew as soon as he said it that nothing was preventing him from doing just that. Did he really need to make a public announcement about it? 'And I don't like girls being with us when we are discussing personal things.' That did not make much sense either, he thought. Was he saying that if there were no girls he would be quite happy to remain in the group? He was floundering. He knew that the presence of Alex and Lola had had little effect on his decision. His short-lived affair with Alex was something of an embarrassment, although neither of them was too concerned now about what had happened. It was not too difficult to keep out of each other's way.

Silas was struggling. He did not know what to say. Luc was not being very helpful although he must be wondering what he was going on about. What had seemed straightforward earlier was becoming less so by the minute. Something was urging him to move on, but there was something else, unidentifiable but equally demanding, that was causing him a problem. Luc was not too sure what Silas meant either by pretentious or personal and assumed that if he said nothing it might become clear. It did not become clear, because although Silas knew what he meant by it he thought that explaining it to Luc would require too many complicating details in what was turning into an unrewarding monologue. The call ended with Luc's unwillingness to enter into any form of dialogue because he continued to think it would be better dealt with by the group. After a few awkward silences they exchanged pleasantries and rang off.

When the group gathered two days later Luc mentioned Silas's decision to give up his weekly visits to the gym. He tried to explain what Silas had said, but no one could make much sense either of Luc's account of it or what Silas meant about coming on days when the others weren't there.

Drago, who had arrived unusually early, made a contribution to the discussion that seemed to have nothing to do with Silas. 'Ever since I was small child I have a dream, the same one. I have it many times. I am on a train. It is just going from the station. But my luggage is on the platform. Sometimes my luggage is on the train, but I am on the platform. When I wake up I am feeling nervous. I think always of a teddy bear I have when I was child. My mother, she told me this, that when I am four, we are going to a holiday and she forgotten to pack it. Maybe it's something with insecurity.' Drago thought for a few moments and then added, 'Maybe it's about missing the boat.'

Corker who was making one of his rare visits paused on his way to the changing room, nodded his head and looking at Drago as he did so said, 'Macbeth does murder sleep.'

Jerry, who had been wondering why Drago was so interested in the meaning of dreams, remembered how once before he had been surprised by something he had said that would have been more understandable had it come from a psychoanalyst. On the previous occasion he thought it had something to do with Benedict's view that they were all on a journey to Lourdes. He said to Corker, who was standing there, looking as if he was waiting to utter another minimally relevant Shakespearian cliché, 'You're right. I agree with you. Something must be keeping him awake at night. His problem could be to do with his conscience. Instead of facing up to what he thinks is troubling him and perhaps discussing it with us he runs away. It's a pity. He should have told us. Childhood memories are seldom forgotten, particularly if they are painful ones, like losing your teddy bear.'

It was not Drago's teddy or what the equivalent of Silas's teddy might have been that Jerry was thinking about but his own earliest memory of being forbidden to enter his mother's bedroom one morning shortly after his fourth birthday. He had not known at the time that his mother was in labour with his brother. He had never forgiven his brother for his sudden intrusion into the relationship he had always had with her. He could not bring himself to explain to the others how his first memory had so profoundly fed into other much later memories of his absent mother which was preventing him from talking about her to the group that morning. He had not discussed her fully with them, although he might have dropped a few hints. It was not a teddy bear, the halfway-house transitional love object between a mother's love and being grown-up, that he missed, he told himself, but his actual mother.

Instead he said, 'When I was at school I was friendly with a boy whose mother had been shot dead by a stray bullet during a bank robbery. It was just before she was about to give birth to him. She was delivered by post-mortem Caesarean section by a surgeon in the casualty department. An anaesthetic or sterilization was unnecessary since his mother was dead, but time was very much of the essence for the unborn baby. The surgeon got on with it before it was too late. The boy had told him how ironic it was, because his mother had been killed in a bank robbery, that he had been delivered by Caesarean section or what medical student humour referred to as "smash-and-grab" surgery. He was taken into care because his father never turned up to claim him. I've always wondered what effect if anything bonding with someone who wasn't his mother and the trauma of his birth might have had on him. I did not know him well enough at the time to ask.'

He did not add that even if he had asked him he would have been none the wiser. He also wondered why he had embellished the story by mentioning the absence of anaesthesia. Did anything to do with mothers automatically remind him of the absence of feeling? It was certainly true of his mother. Absence of feeling was not exclusive to dead mothers. Death might be the ultimate anaesthetic, but his mother was still alive, although so far as he was concerned she had been dead, emotionally at least, for years.

It came to Jerry, suddenly out of the blue, that for the first time he understood why he had been depressed on and off for as long as he could remember. He was mourning the loss of his mother. It was hardly surprising that his school friend's story had made such an impression on him. Shut out of her bedroom at the age of four, he had been shut out of her life ever since.

Corker had just managed to say that something similarly untimely had happened to Macduff at his birth, when to the groups's surprise Silas suddenly arrived and said, 'Hi. How's everyone?'

Everyone greeted him as if they had no idea that he had decided not to come any more. Puzzled, they tried not to show their bewilderment. Silas had at last got their attention. He had finally convinced himself after a sleepless night that, although Luc had probably told them of his decision, he did not want to miss out on telling them himself. He hoped he wasn't making a mistake. It wouldn't be the first time that he had acted in haste and later regretted it. He had remained uncertain even after his arrival at the gym. He had remained out of sight, although not out of earshot, for a good ten minutes before he could bring himself to put on a face as cheerful as he was capable of and greet them.

In that ten minutes he thought about all the women he had loved and left. One of them would probably have been all right if he had hung on for a bit longer. He knew what he was doing was much of the same. He tried to reassure himself that missing out did not have to be a pattern that could never be changed. He could always return to the group if he changed his mind. What had Jerry said about the boy whose mother was dead when he was born? At least his own mother was alive when he was born, even though he would have been dead if she'd had her way and had an abortion. Perhaps he shouldn't have spent so much of his life misrepresenting himself as an orphan, as someone unloved and unwanted. His mother had existed, and more than that she had looked after him, perhaps not in the way he would have preferred, but at least he was here to complain about it. Blaming others can't be the answer; neither can representing oneself as unwanted, particularly if all he was intent on was to check if he actually was.

He had no idea what the group thought about him. They might actually like him. He wondered whether he was having second thoughts. Perhaps he should try to elaborate on what he was going to say. They had been together for several years, and it seemed discourteous to leave without explaining how he felt. Anyway, getting their attention was something of an achievement.

'Luc might have told you. I'm giving up the gym. Not completely. I'll probably come on Tuesdays instead. It will give me more time for sculpting. I've got a gallery very interested in my work as it happens.'

He knew this was untrue, but he liked the sound of it. He wondered if he should leave it at that or tell them about his unwillingness to join in the social activities in which they were all becoming involved. Perhaps he had said enough. They would soon find out, as he thought he had found out, that there was something rotten in the state of Denmark. Would he have said that before? He didn't think so. Anyway did he really think some evil was going on somewhere that was affecting his life? It was years since he had even thought about Hamlet. Of course nothing evil was going on. It was a quote he had picked up in the group and was carrying around with him. Corker had been more influential than he could have imagined. Could he be carrying away anything else he had failed to recognize? He had barely registered Corker's lifetime involvement with Shakespeare. Perhaps there had been other comments or patterns of thinking with which he had been impressed without realizing it.

No one had acted in the way he had. No one had decided to leave the group suddenly without telling anyone. When Ed stopped coming he had made some excuse or other that didn't even lead to a discussion. Everyone sooner or later had to accept responsibility for themselves. He would have liked to have known how Jerry's friend turned out. Maybe he was now happily married with two kids. He could not dine out for ever on the hardships of his upbringing. Perhaps it is worth giving something a try even when everything seems hopeless. The casualty surgeon took that view with Jerry's friend's mother. There's life in the old dog yet. The surgeon must have thought that, and he was right.

It reminded him of the painting of the dog who was barely keeping his head above water. It was the photo he kept on his mobile. The dog had not drowned. The artist had painted him with his head above water, not below it. Had he given up too soon? Perhaps he should have done the doggy paddle and headed for shore. That was another interpretation of the painting. He might have kept it on his phone for the wrong reason. He was always misinterpreting things. Silas felt slightly uneasy. Maybe there was something else that had made him give up. Maybe he should explain himself rather more fully. They were looking at him. Expectantly or not he did not know.

'There's another thing. Our discussions. It's the only thing that makes the exercises less boring. But I'm not too keen on the social side.'

'The other group has a social side,' said Jerry. 'They get a free lunch every Friday. Not entirely free. They pay something, but very little. They enjoy the soup and salad. One or two of them don't even bother with the exercises. They just come for the lunch.'

'That's my point. They just come for lunch. It has nothing to do with what they talk about. It's not connected with anything else. It's just lunch. They eat it and go home.'

'No such thing as a free lunch,' Harold said.

'Someone always has to pay,' Jerry added. 'It's probably one of the laws of economics. Anyway, most people value only what they pay for. Freebies are put in the bin, although, come to think of it, we do get a lot of feedback when we go out for lunch. It's when we exchange information with one another,' he explained in case Silas had lost him.

Silas was becoming irritated. They were not listening to what he was trying to tell them. They were more involved in metaphor which would keep them happily engaged until it was time to start the exercises. But what was he trying to tell them? He was becoming confused. Why was he giving up?

Benedict, whose thoughts seldom strayed far from his interest in churches and spires and their design and who had been half listening but had so far said nothing, suddenly spoke up. 'It's like the Tower of Pisa. The main reason that millions of people come to see it is not that it's been there for 700 years or so or because it's a World Heritage Site, or even because it's a reasonably attractive tower, but because it leans more to one side than perhaps any other tower in the world. Everyone loves it because it's an architectural cock-up. A 'capital-out-of-error' phenomenon. Nothing is ever quite what it seems. There has to be more to everything than just a free lunch.'

The group perked up, although not everyone seemed to be sure what Benedict actually meant by the last bit.

Jerry was about to say that if anyone was familiar with architectural cock-ups it had to be Benedict but thought better of it and remarked, 'What about the recently minted 20p coins that don't have the date on them? They're worth £100 each. The Mint is trying to locate them and buy them back. There has never been so much interest in a 20p piece since they came into existence.'

The group became suddenly excited by examples of how when the spotlight falls unintentionally it may not necessarily be on the deserving. Silas faded them out, but he knew if anyone had been faded out it was him. That was typical. That was one of the things that annoyed him. Benedict always did that. He probably did it on purpose just to be clever. What was the error that he was supposed to be making capital out of? He didn't know. But what if Benedict was right? He was already beginning to wonder if he was making a mistake. If he was, it had to be an unforced error, as they would say in tennis. No one had made him do it. What he was now worrying about was who was going to make capital out of what might be his error. He wandered off against a background of upside-down watermarks on postage stamps and literary misquotations. No one noticed he had gone.

TWENTY-FOUR

&

Harold had been listening with increasing anxiety to Silas's concerns about the group. His decision to leave made him almost as uneasy as it seemed to have made Silas. Did he have a guilty secret? Was that the real reason he wanted to give up? It couldn't possibly be through pressure of work. He was always complaining that he didn't have any. Had he invented that story because he did not want to tell anyone the real reason? What could he be hiding from them? Was it possible they shared the same problem? Had Silas guessed that he, too, had something to hide? Could he have known what it was? That would be terrible. If he did know about his problem, it was a blessing that he would not be coming any more. Harold felt ever more panicky, and his thinking was becoming increasingly circular. He was able to reassure himself for much of the time that Silas could not possibly have guessed what was on his mind, but he knew that as soon as he began thinking about how unattractive a certain part of his body was he would be stuck with his fear of discovery for hours, maybe days. He must find something to take his mind off it.

He remembered that he had always worried before about something slipping out, particularly if it was his penis. It had not slipped out yet. It was quite funny how certain words like that had become a feature of his thinking. He would love to tell someone and make them laugh. He could be a stand-up comic. That was funny, too. Perhaps he should stop worrying about it so much and treat it as a joke. He did not think it strange that it seemed to be for ever in his mind. It seemed natural that it should be. Perhaps one day he would get used to it and just accept it. He had managed to get used to being a don with an interest in something he knew absolutely nothing about. Since none of the others knew anything about it either, it was unlikely to come up. That was another slip of the tongue. He laughed again. He began to feel much better. Harold thought about the friends he had made at the gym. He always looked forward to making his contributions to the discussions. He had learned a lot from them, but unlike Silas he had no wish to give up any of it.

He was a solitary person. He could not really be otherwise. Not with the problem he had. He had been wondering recently whether surgery might be the answer. He had often thought about it, but it was too frightening to consider seriously. It was only his preoccupation that had made him want to keep it to himself. When it was not on his mind he was as chatty as anyone else. It was true that he had been reluctant to speak last week when they were talking about a sex problem that someone's GP had said was caused by one of the pills he was taking. Whenever he thought of anything becoming too close for comfort he kept silent and waited for one of the others to change the subject. He would hate it if someone were to ask him what his views were about anything so personal.

Silas's concern that the group had lost something by being too revelatory made no sense to him. Knowing what the others did or where they lived or whether they were gay or straight, rich or poor, young or old did not change how he felt about them. They were his friends, and he could see that the more they came to know one another the stronger their friendship became. Silas seemed to think that knowing who the others were detracted from whatever he was getting out of it.

It occurred to him that perhaps Silas was experiencing the group as a therapy group. He knew about therapy groups. He had been in one some years earlier when he'd had panic attacks. It was when he had first had his problem. The therapy group had not helped him with it. It was the last thing he had wanted to talk about. But he remembered that he had enjoyed going, and it did help him relate better in social situations.

He had been self-conscious since he was very young; it had stopped him from having many friends while he was growing up. Not much different now, he thought. The therapy group had been a great comfort. There were others to talk to who listened. He also listened and would often make helpful suggestions. But none of them went out to lunch together when the group was over. Come to think of it, they were given specific instructions not to meet outside. It had something to do with what they discussed. Some of it had to do with members of their families and how some issues could only be addressed and understood within the group because it had become a family unit itself. They could then rethink what had upset them earlier in life and share their feelings and experiences in a setting that was confidential and in which no one would be offended. The therapist had told them that meeting socially might interfere with that.

The gym group did support one another and confided in one another, but they also had lunch together. Harold saw nothing wrong in that. He did not think about it as a therapy group like the one that had helped him become more sociable. Otherwise he would have just come to the gym, done the exercises and gone home as soon as it was over. He would not want to do another therapy group. Most people had something to hide. For some it might just be something about which they were self-conscious, like the problem he had, and for others it might be something mildly antisocial. None of the others seemed to be anything other than well-meaning inhabitants of the world in which they lived. But it was all a matter of degree. It was difficult for everyone to keep to the letter of anything. His mind wandered off to the rules laid down by religious teaching. The group often talked about it – like the Ten Commandments or the Sermon on the Mount. They considered them as merely recommendations of do's and don'ts. They did not agree with fundamentalists who took them literally as God-given absolutes.

Some religious laws had provided a field day for psycho-analysts. He agreed that envy was undesirable. He did envy something. But Freud had got it wrong as far as he was concerned. He'd had the idea that all men suffered from a fear of being castrated. Freud had put this down to what boys of about four believed would happen to them if they did not give up competing with their father for sex with their mother. Harold thought it quite ridiculous to believe that a small boy would even be thinking about sex with his mother, never mind considering planning it. Freud wrote that boys were terrified when they discovered that their sisters did not have a penis. They assumed that they must already have been castrated. Harold thought that sounded more like poetry than psychology. Freud also said that girls envied boys their penis and wished they had one. It was nonsense as far as he was concerned. He definitely did not envy a man his penis and probably never had since he was not a girl anyway. On the contrary, he envied girls their lack of a penis. He did not suffer from castration anxiety. He would have been far less anxious if he had been castrated.

He started thinking about girls and penises. He knew that some girls like Alex behaved as if they had one. She seemed very bossy, very much a tomboy. But did he envy her that aspect of her behaviour? He was not sure. He liked the idea that she did not have a penis, although, if Freud was right, she may once have wished she'd had one. He liked the fact that she was a girl and not a man. He liked her but not enough to want to be involved with her. He decided that intimacy was the last thing he wanted with anyone. Privacy was his passion, not intimacy.

TWENTY-FIVE

෴

Alex and Lola had not joined in the discussion that accompanied Silas's rather staged farewell that morning. They were as surprised as everyone else by his sudden and unexpected appearance so soon after Luc's announcement that he would no longer be coming on the days the group was there. Both young women had taken a view as to why Silas had made his decision to give up, but neither of them believed that he had been entirely honest either with himself or with the rest of them. Neither of them wanted to share their views with the others.

On their way home from the gym, Alex said, 'There's something fishy going on. I can't believe that he's making such a big issue out of it. If he's got something better to do, then he should just get on with it and do it. No one would even notice that he hadn't been around for a while. Someone might eventually ask whether anyone's seen him but certainly not before a month or two. You know how people are. He's making a point that doesn't need to be made.' After a pause while she gathered her thoughts she added, 'I get the feeling that grandiosity has a lot to do with it. He's achieved what he probably set out to do. That is that we should be talking about him. I'm sure he's pleased that we are all wondering what it's all about. It's just a way of grabbing attention.'

Lola, as ever the passive follower rather than the active leader, slipped into the role she believed Alex expected her to play. It was a listening, understanding and supportive role, a role with which she was fed up. She registered Alex's irritation at Silas's behaviour and acknowledged to herself that she was hardly surprised by it, although she was concerned that Alex seemed a bit worked up by it. She was not displeased, however, by Alex coming across as hostile about her lover. She just hoped her hostility was genuine. 'What do you think he's up to?'

'He's just trying to make us feel guilty. He can see that most of the others, and I suppose to a lesser extent us as well, have formed a friendship that he is incapable of entering into because being part of a family unit is outside his experience. He may want one since he's never had one, but he does not want anyone else to have one, so he is trying to sabotage us. I wouldn't mind betting that he'll soon think of other ways of doing that. He has to be in control. He's not going to give that up. He feels safer when he calls the shots. It's like someone who has a flying phobia knowing that if he were flying the aircraft his phobia would cease to exist. He doesn't trust the pilot. I don't think he trusts anyone. He probably doesn't even trust himself. It must have come to a head at Benedict's lunch. The person in charge then, if it was anyone, was Benedict. It must be Benedict he's got it in for.' Varying her metaphors slightly to add emphasis to her theory, she continued, 'Anyone rowing the boat, other than himself, would make him feel very unsafe.' She paused and thought for a moment. 'And anyone in charge of feeding arrangements must, symbolically at least, be the mother.'

She was pleased with her interpretation of the changes that she thought were taking place in the group. She was not sure whether she was right in her analysis of the situation, but she knew that she was disappointed that her audience consisted of no one but Lola. She would have preferred to have had a wider audience, particularly if it included Benedict, whom she was still trying to impress, so far without success. She was sure that she loved Lola. But that was different. She loved her with the caring, affectionate side of herself, not with the erotic side with which she had been carried away with Silas. Lola was well rounded in more ways than one, but she wished she was intellectually as sharp as most of the men. It was not always easy to keep up with them. Sometimes it took hours before she realized that what sounded inconsequential was actually something totally relevant. You needed to understand their language. It was not so much what they said but, often, what lay behind it. It didn't do to be too literal. Jerry was pointed and sometimes cutting. Harold and Drago were often totally incomprehensible. Luc was the only one who seemed warm and cuddly. But they all, including Silas, until he decided to call it a day, seemed able to tune into what any one of the others were saying. Would she exchange Lola for any of them? Rhetorical questions could be difficult. She could not have everything, but she would not object if she could.

Alex did not know how any of them felt about Silas leaving. They kept their thoughts to themselves. She was beginning to come to the conclusion that Silas might have felt that they were in what might be turning out to be a therapy group which had broken an unspoken rule that socializing of any kind outside the group would inevitably lead to its collapse. She would have been surprised to know that Harold had already considered that as a possibility. Benedict had been there that morning but chose not to express an opinion, more's the pity, she thought, and of the others Jerry and Drago were their baffling selves. She found it hard to tie in Corker's obsession with *Macbeth*, and Luc was, as ever, all things to all men.

She was left to work it out for herself. She felt that she knew Silas better than any of them, and she had physical intimacy to fall back on. None of the others had that. In the short time they had spent together she and Silas had never kept anything to themselves. She was as familiar with his background and his outlook on life as only a lover could be. How difficult it must be for anyone to remain detached in the presence of such closeness. She was, of course, not Silas's therapist, much as he might have liked her to be. Neither was she his mistress. He had not kept her. If anything she had spent more on the relationship than he. His need to be provided for had proved to be expensive. In other respects they were equal partners, and, during what now seemed to have been only for a moment, their love for one another could not have been more intense nor their enjoyment of recreational sex, which they had confused with intellectual understanding, never more pressing.

She no longer thought of Silas as a lover but a saboteur. It was obvious to her now that he was envious of the happiness of others and was convinced that everyone in the group was having a better time than he. He had not wanted to talk about much of that to her. When she confronted him with the happiness or the prosperity of any of the others he would sulk for a while but then recover. Now it had gone beyond that. He had given up speaking to them or contributing to their activities and ultimately had run away from everyone and anything that reminded him of what he believed they had but he didn't. He may have run away, but Alex knew that he looked over his shoulder to see who was running after him. He wanted his pursuer to catch up and ask him to return.

It may well have been true that no one had ever loved him, but she could not help resenting his attitude to that fact. His belief in his loveless background was strong, but she felt that he was old enough neither to need ongoing proof, nor to feel pleased when the others discovered that they also lacked something similar. She was not worried about Silas's decision. What did worry her was that, because envy was so destructive, Silas might do his best, perhaps unwittingly, to break up the group, which he believed embodied the rejection he had been brought up to expect. It had not taken her long to realize that far from representing a rejecting family, the group was more of a listening, accepting and thoughtful support for all of them.

Lola's thoughts were different. She was happy to find herself once again walking side by side, if not hand in hand, with the woman she loved and hoping that in the absence of her rival their relationship would be given another opportunity to flourish. She was determined to share her life with Alex. Ever since that evening when they had declared their love for one another, momentous for her but she feared possibly less so for Alex, she had anxiously surveyed the landscape for any sign of competition.

She was reminded of the first time she had become aware that she and Alex were attracted to one another. She was shocked when she discovered that their feelings were sexual, although she was conscious of occasional fleeting feelings over and above those which two sixteen-year-olds might have had towards each other.

They had been walking home from school one day, each of them heartened by the feeling that there was someone with whom they could share their problems. Arriving at a T-junction they were just about to part when Alex said, 'I don't think I'll ever get over my mother's death.'

What Alex was looking for was sympathy and understanding, but what she received from Lola was much more gratifying. She had put her arms around Alex and hugged her. The spontaneity and the warmth of her response brought tears to Alex's eyes. Lola also began to cry, not so much because of the loss of her friend's mother, something she had never been allowed to forget, but out of sympathy for Alex. The two girls felt something pass between them which neither could identify. Slowly Alex had withdrawn from the embrace and they stood facing one another, flushed with embarrassment.

Standing at the end of the lane with the daylight fading, they had kissed each other briefly but with a passion that neither of them had before experienced. Clinging so closely that their bodies felt fused, Lola remembered walking home as in a dream that promised something she thought she would never have. Ten years later she still hoped that a woman's love would one day be available to her and that the magic of that moment would be repeated.

Sometimes she saw the group as a rival. Although she knew she did not have the intuitive awareness of some of the others she realized that its members were not really in competition with her or with one another but seemed to relate as concerned friends might.

She was reassured by what a friend had once told her of what life as a medical student was like. The students became a 'family'. Her friend said they needed one another because they were away from home for the first time and saw each other as an extension of the support system they had grown up with. They helped one another cope with illness, exams and loneliness. A physical relationship with other 'family' members was never on the cards. They had to grow up and leave home before intimacy was possible. Lola could see that shared involvement with matters of life and death might draw medical students to shelter in a family-style unit, but it seemed not to apply to either her or Alex. It was very much like how the others in the gym group except for Silas behaved. She wondered what made them group together. She and Alex were not really family members. Silas was, but he kept running away, testing to see if they loved him.

The group was not her family. She was rather pleased it was not. She would be more than happy to be physically involved with her friend. Alex also did not belong, although Lola knew she would like to.

Medical students might evolve in an information-only nursery where overexposure to everything left no room for privacy, but Lola thought that the same could be true of any other hothouse. She was convinced that if people came together in any common cause they would eventually turn into a family. It did not take long for members of a choir to end up singing from the same song sheet or battle-weary soldiers to become brothers in arms. Sooner or later, unless they escaped, Alex would become her sister. That was the last thing she wanted. It might be all right for the very old. All passion spent. They may not be too bothered by any of that. But she was.

Lola felt she must tell Alex that she was beginning to feel the group oppressive. It was becoming too close for comfort. Staying in or breaking out – as Jerry had described it at Benedict's lunch – was becoming a real consideration. She knew she was devaluing the group. Would that make it easier to give it up?

It was not long since she and Alex had discussed their disappointment at being ignored by the men. They had desperately wanted to join them, and it was only because of Alex's sudden involvement with Silas that they had been accepted. They had wanted in. Now they wanted out. Recognition had been the poisoned chalice that opened the door, but it had also locked it behind them. She told Alex she was becoming stir crazy. Silas must have felt as she did. Was he now leading a mad rush for the exit? Did he know something she didn't?

Lola did not like her friend's reaction to Silas's departure. She remembered her passionate falling-in-hate with him. Could it be that she would miss him? Maybe it was more than that. She may no longer like him, but was she too preoccupied with him? There might still be unfinished business between them. Lola had become so anxious about losing her friend that she had forgotten that one of the things that really upset Alex was anyone walking away from her. She must not feel entirely convinced that it was she not he who had terminated their brief fling. That must be it. Walking away seemed to be the order of the day. Maybe it was not Silas who had started the break-up. It might just be because the group had become time-expired. Is that how she felt about it? It could not go on for ever. Lola and Alex were supposed to be starting their so-called sabbatical soon. They seemed to have forgotten that.

They were signs that they might be escaping, but she worried that Alex might have yet another agenda to address. Alex was attracted to Benedict, but there was nothing to suggest that her feelings were reciprocated. He ignored her. The more Lola thought about him, the more she realized that his emotions were entirely taken up by his work. His work was the love of his life, not women, not men, but dreaming spires. She was relieved. All artists had to be passionate about their creativity, otherwise they turned out to be run of the mill or, as Alex sometimes said when at an inferior Italian restaurant, run of the pepper mill.

TWENTY-SIX

꧁

Benedict had been in Italy for a few days and was telling everyone how he had felt when he visited his cousin's fish farm in Sardinia. 'I've not been able to eat fish since. It was awful, but I can't quite understand why I felt so badly about it.'

'I don't like to eat the battery chicken,' Drago said. 'I don't think about the battery fish.'

'This was different.' He wasn't sure why it was different but he needed to share with the group how he felt. 'The farm was on the bank of a river just as it ran into the sea. The fish in the tanks are fed with food made partly from fish maybe of their own species but probably also other fish too small for human consumption. All this is mixed with various chemicals presumably thought to be good for them. Some of it gets into the river, and as the tide comes in a huge mass of other fish crowd into the river and fight each other for the farm fishes' leftovers. There's something about this frenzied feeding I found very distressing. There were so many fish. I've never seen anything like it.'

As he said this Benedict remembered that he had been in a restaurant once when a couple at the next table had asked whether he was going to eat the remainder of his steak and if not could they have it? He had thought at the time that there might be something environmentally sound about not wasting food, although it was certainly socially questionable, but he had thought nothing more about it. Leftovers from a rich man's table, the fishes struggle for

191

survival, immigrants struggling to reach a promised land inhabited by a privileged few. What had made him think of that? It was not the fish or the diners in the restaurant but immigration that stayed in his mind. Was he part of a struggle to find a life somewhere? Feeling sorry for fish and giving up eating them was not going to help him achieve that. Maybe he had not left his past behind him after all. He had certainly been moved by what he had seen.

He was having a struggle to survive, work was in short supply and he was having a bad moment. He resented being reminded of Silas's decision to give up the gym and wondered whether he was trying to sabotage the group. Why are all of us so involved with Silas and his problems? We talk about him and possibly think about him more since he's left than we did while he was here.

He had just decided to throw this thought open to discussion when Jerry, who was still thinking about the fish, said, 'They can't help being cannibals. They may eat one another in their regular habitat. Big fish have always eaten smaller fish. Are you worrying about the bullying aspect of it? Big teeth are definitely aggressive. But the question seems to be why you are so affected by it. Clearly cannibalism, if that's what you feel it might be, is a major taboo. There was that air crash years ago in Chile in which some people survived by eating those who hadn't. I would think the example you describe, though, has more to do with the wish to make a better life for ourselves.'

What Jerry was saying was valid. Benedict was beginning to understand why one of nature's less agreeable features had affected him so badly but could not bring himself to reason it through any further and commented, 'The fish seemed to be actually fighting one another. Some looked quite bizarre. It was quite frightening.'

'You should not worry about it. Wild salmon.' Drago said. 'They are swimming half round the world to get back where they come from. Soon they are big and strong with big fins. Not like farmed ones. It's the exercise. We look like farmed fish if we do not come to the gym.'

But Benedict did worry about it. He returned to the image of the swirling mass of fish struggling and fighting. Was it really how he saw himself? Was it a reminder of what might have been? It was he who had been going nowhere fast. For some time he had felt he was one of the struggling masses, a reminder that he had made it but millions had not.

He was still standing on the bank looking at what had been and what still might be but not at what was. Drago was right from that point of view. We would all look like that if we didn't come to the gym. Benedict knew it was not just the gym. It was what they also came for. All of them in the group, even the one who did not want to come any more, the one who had not sat on the empty chair in the Chinese restaurant. Jerry suddenly realized that it was not Silas who might cause the group to break up. Silas was part of the cement that held them together. It was his awful background and Jerry's awful mother and other as yet unexplored 'awfuls' including his own. Silas had needed to be with them more than anyone. He seemed to have been the one against whom they tested themselves. He was at best a mirror and at worst a representation of failure to recognize the role they were playing.

Benedict thought Silas probably knew he needed the group. But being reminded of happy families rather than the unhappy one he was used to distressed him. He had been unable to cope with discovering what he had missed out on, particularly when exposed to the obvious harmony of the others. He might not only have spoiled it for everyone else but also for himself. He may not have realized he was doing that. Benedict thought: he will return because he left before he was ready.

Silas, the subject of Benedict's thoughts, was sitting at home feeling miserable. He had blown it. Why did he always have to fulfil his own prophesy that the world was full of people who did not like him? It was not the first time. He had done it with every girl he had dated, whether he had picked them up in pubs or on the internet. And he had behaved so badly with his wife that no one could have blamed her for leaving him. He had even been like that at school. He had never had many friends, and looking back he could see why. He had not bothered with them. All he wanted to be was teacher's pet and, as time passed, anyone else's pet. He could see now why that never went down too well. If anyone needed the companionship of the group, particularly the family aspect of it, he did. He had sensed it but had decided to walk away from it. He could not wait for the inevitability of rejection. Had he known that everyone thought about him much of the time and liked him, and also talked frequently about his leaving, about which they all had a theory, he would not have believed it.

He might have been cheered to know how much he was missed, but the way things were going he was not going to find out. What was he to do? He liked the gym, he liked the group, he liked a lot of the people in the other group as well, and he also liked one of the trainers who had the same sense of humour, he thought gloomily (that is if he still possessed it), as he had. All that was now gone, and he had done it not to the group as had been his intention but to himself. He could not have done much more damage to his hopes and aspirations if he had blown them up with a hand grenade. He went over in his mind about how he felt about the friends he had made in the gym, hoping to find some justification for what he had done. It would at least be some sort of comfort if he knew it was because he could not stand some of them or that one had been particularly offensive to him. But he could think of no one he even mildly disliked. He thought Jerry's interpretations of what people said to him were occasionally over the top and Benedict could often be dismissive, but Luc was easy to get on with and he liked Drago. Harold was a bit odd and so was Corker. The two girls were a special case, and he and Alex had wrong-footed one another, but that was now history and no lasting harm had been done.

Why, then, had he told them he was no longer coming? It was true he was a bit hard up, but others managed it. Was he too sensitive? In his happier moments he realized that he was more than just a little paranoid, but he was trying to deal with it. He knew that if he believed no one liked him he would go on testing that belief until he was proved right. He was aware of what he had done, but how could he reverse it? He might try to keep in touch with some of them and see what came of it. Perhaps they had come to a similar conclusion about him. He went down to the pub to think it over.

TWENTY-SEVEN

❦

Luc was surprised when he received a text from Silas a few days later. He did not expect to feel surprised because what others might be able to respond to at once often took a while to sink in for him. He considered everything very carefully before he allowed himself to react emotionally to anything. He put it down to his decision, impulsive at the time but disastrous in the event, to join the Foreign Legion so many years ago only to leave equally impulsively after just a month. He had never been able to forget it, never forgiven himself for it and regretted having told the group about a decision which had affected his outlook on life. Spontaneous and open might have described him before he had abandoned his commitment. Now it was just a front. He had got into the habit of appearing that way at the gym. He did not want anyone to know that he was putting on a good face to give him time to consider what was said to him, time to prevent him from commenting unwisely on whatever was being discussed, time to prevent his guilt feelings slipping out. Overcoming the self-reproach that never left him took up most of his waking moments.

Misleading the military authorities, he had convinced himself, was the most serious of all offences committed by a serving soldier, even one with as short a record as his. Always on his mind, he had felt compelled to confess to his friends at the gym. As genuine liberal thinkers they believed that the French should not have been fighting to hold on to their colonies in the first place. He knew they would be sympathetic and understanding, and they certainly were. In a way it had been a relief. Jerry had even said that he should be regarded as a hero for having been brave enough to walk away from unjust wars. At the time he had no idea whether they were unjust or not. He simply did not want to be there. He was no hero, but there was certainly bravery involved, or more likely bravado, because he knew at the time what the penalty was if he was caught lying to the authorities. It might be history now, but as far as Luc was concerned the law, or his conscience at least, had a very long arm. He told everyone who might have noticed his hesitancy that it was because his knowledge of English was not as good as he would have liked. But it was not that. His English was as good as anyone's. It was mainly down to his sense of impending doom, his ever-present feeling of guilt, of discovery and had nothing to do with being a slow and guarded thinker.

If it was to do with anything, other than running away from his duties, it was to do with sex. Whenever a new woman came into his life and sex was on offer he had been an immediate responder. He would react first and think about it later. Now such behaviour made him feel angry with himself. Looking back he could see that the need to gratify his sex drive had taken up so much time and energy that it had seriously diminished the time available to him for other activities. He thought that a high sex drive was fine when population increase was a survival imperative. Contraception had switched sex into a recreational activity and not only for men. Today women were using their surplus energy for purposes that years ago would not have been possible.

Sex was supposed to make you feel good, but it had never brought him happiness. If anything it had brought the opposite. A brief high to which it was easy to become addicted and then a long unhappy period while he thought about the distress he was causing often to the partner of one of his conquests. Fortunately for him Véronique had been divorced when he met her. She was the last of his mistresses and would remain the last. He had not actually married her. That would have been asking for trouble. Marriage was the cause of all his problems. He enjoyed it briefly and then felt trapped, so he escaped. Commitment was the last thing he wanted. As soon as achieved it he would look for a way out. He did not want anyone to know how many times he had been married. He was too embarrassed. He could scarcely remember himself. He had loved Véronique and would never have cheated on her, unless of course he had married her.

What was that all about? He asked himself. He must try to find out one day. It's not too late. He might ask Jerry or maybe Benedict. He had worked out that being enclosed anywhere from which he could not easily escape – a lift stuck between floors, a train that had broken down in a tunnel, a marriage or anywhere where his freedom was threatened – made him panic. He did not feel like that when he was in control. It was probably why he had given up the army in the first place. It had nothing to do with patriotism or French colonialism. That was pure invention to impress the others. It was because he had felt trapped by the terms and conditions of his employment. He was not in control of anything during that month. To remain on guard duty for four hours was only one of the many situations with which he had been unable to cope and which had led to unbearable panic.

He hoped that Silas was not going to make demands on him. He did not want to be pinned down by anything or anyone ever again. He must have given him the impression that he was to be relied upon. He would try to seem more indifferent in future. As far as he was concerned Silas had come, amused them briefly and then gone. He could live with that. But leaving messages to call him back was too much. Why had Silas become so attached to him? As far as he knew he had not tried to contact any of the others. Had Silas tuned into a caring side of himself that he wasn't aware he had. He was no agony aunt and had no intention of becoming one. Most of the others thought they were agony aunts. Why didn't he call one of them? Jerry would have sorted him out. Perhaps that was why he hadn't asked him. Silas had never given anyone the impression that he was expecting help with whatever might have gone wrong in his life. He must have problems, but Luc had no idea what they were or how he would be able to help him with them. Most of the group seemed to think that it was because no one saw Silas as their natural leader, but he was not sure about that.

He had listened to the others discussing why Silas had decided to leave, but none of it meant much. He was not particularly impressed with their reasoning either. They had certainly got him wrong. If that was how they saw him it was because that was how they wanted to see him. He had learned that much by listening to their discussions, much of which he did not understand anyway.

If anything he was rather irritated by Silas because although he understood only too well – probably better than any of the others, come to think of it – that nothing lasted for ever, he had settled into a comfortable, companionable relationship with everyone. Silas's defection had altered what he had come to expect and invariably looked forward to on the two days a week that he came to the gym.

Silas could well be having real problems, but if so they were problems that had nothing to do with him. He might even be regretting that he had been so hasty. At least someone might have been able to help with whatever was bothering him. Luc had no clear idea of why Silas had decided to call it a day; neither did it occur to him that he might be being used as a bridge to reconnect him to the others, a halfway house that would allow a tentative approach to be made without committing him to anything.

He thought he had better call him back. The phone rang just once. He felt as if Silas had been waiting for his call. It was as if the swiftness with which the phone had been answered had added urgency to the situation. Silas was pressurizing him. It made him even more anxious about something with which he had not wanted to be involved in the first place.

Silas said, 'Do you feel like coming for a walk in the park? Maybe we could have a sandwich or something.'

Luc thought for a moment, looked at his watch and said, 'OK. Where shall we go?'

'Let's not bother with the park. How about Franco's? It's not much further to walk, and they know us there.' Silas always liked to be somewhere where he was known. He had come to recognize that this was a feature of his personality. Wanting to be acknowledged, welcomed, greeted and invited to sit down in what was, after all, a simple sandwich bar where the manager, for reasons known only to himself, wanted him to feel at home made Silas feel needed.

Luc was happy with this suggestion. He and Franco would exchange a few words in French, a language that he seldom used and which Franco hardly knew. It reminded him of home. It reminded him of his father; the chef who had taught him to think of cooking as an art.

He found Silas more amiable, more talkative and much warmer than he had been recently. Ever aware of how one chose to present oneself, Luc wondered which was the real Silas and which the one for public consumption. After ordering food as far removed from the panini that the group invariably chose, they agreed on two cups of tea, a Florentine biscuit for Silas, who had lost his appetite, and a roast-beef baguette for Luc and settled down, one to talk and one to listen.

'Well, what do you think?' said Silas.

Luc thought: This is just typical. He's assuming that I've thought of nothing else since he announced his resignation. Luc wondered why his thinking was becoming slightly grandiose. Announcing his resignation! 'Had decided to give up coming to the gym' was more appropriate. Had he caught something from one of the others? He dragged his thoughts back to Silas. If he's expecting me to provide a full rundown on what everyone thinks about him he's going to be disappointed. He smiled benignly and said smoothly, 'What do I think about what?'

Silas didn't reply, and Luc was beginning to feel that he had offended him when suddenly Silas started to talk about the others as they appeared to him. He had talked to himself about them on many occasions but repeatedly chewing over the same thing had not made it more palatable. It simply meant that the topic in hand might be rather less hard to swallow. Talking to someone other than himself would obviously be much better. He had got very little feedback from talking to himself about any of the complaints and problems he had with each and every one of them. Now that he had an audience it was another matter. Something to get his teeth into. He wondered whether he had caught his metaphorical thinking from Corker, who had obviously caught it from being too close to Shakespeare, in particular *Macbeth*.

Although Luc and the two girls were not included for obvious reasons, Silas managed to badmouth every other member of the group. It was as if he was mentally ticking them off from a list he had been carrying around for a long time. Luc gave up listening after a few minutes when it became obvious that the complaints were all of a piece. The thread that ran through it all was that he was being ignored, that people were ganging up on him and that they all had ideas about themselves and each other, as well as the group and its make-up, with which he did not agree.

Luc thought how strange it was that Silas was taking far more interest in the others than he had ever taken when he came regularly. It was becoming obvious that the role of outsider, as Luc put it to himself, was not one that suited him. He would have been surprised to know that the term meant socially unacceptable as well as not belonging. He would have been even more surprised if he had known that was exactly how Silas had thought about himself ever since his mother had told him that she would have had an abortion if his father had told her he was leaving, before it was too late for one to be carried out.

TWENTY-EIGHT

Alex and Lola were pushing their trolley around the supermarket when Lola, bored with the shopping, tried to convince herself that something might come of her relationship with Alex after all. She could not bring herself to put it into words. It might be unlucky. There was something about it that was still very fragile. She dared not ask Alex what she thought. She could not rid herself of her fear that Alex might still be waiting for something better to come along. Although she thought that Alex probably did love her, Lola was well aware that her friend was an opportunist. What she really needed to know was whether Alex was a committed lesbian. She had to admit that she did not think she was, although she had been very responsive on the one occasion when they had made love. They had agreed that they were in love with one another. She sighed. She hoped it was a good omen that she was talking about giving up the gym. It was only yesterday that they had begun to discuss their travel plans again which had been on hold for months.

Her thoughts were interrupted by Alex asking, 'What did you really think about that lunch Benedict gave in his garden?'

Lola was surprised by the question, not because there might be something sinister that could be read into it but because it clashed with what was going on in her head. She found it a wrench to break off from thinking about making love with Alex. She had been wondering whether she could do something practical about it immediately or at least as soon as they got home that afternoon. They had nothing planned, nothing outdoors anyway, since it was raining. But having to talk about Benedict was definitely not on her agenda. She dragged herself away from her fantasy to the less attractive image of the builder's yard. She focused her attention on a fish counter as they passed by on which 'catch of the day' fish lay seductively on a bed of ice. She hoped it might take her mind off her thoughts. Instead it seemed paradoxically to enhance them.

She managed to say, 'It was OK. Why do you ask?'

'You're right. It was OK. But only just. We could have done it much better.'

It was not what Alex was saying that concerned Lola. It was how she was saying it. She recognized an expression on her friend's face, a certain tone in her voice, something that was there only when she was up to no good. What did she have in mind? 'I agree. Of course we could, but since we live in a minute flat it might be rather difficult.'

Alex looked at Lola. 'What about Aunt Daphne?'

Lola knew about Daphne, Alex's late mother's sister. She and Alex were very close. She was as near to a mother to Alex as anyone other than an actual mother could be. Alex had often told her that she was sometimes even nearer. When she was a child Daphne had always been on her side when family issues or decisions about schools were up for discussion. Now she was an adult and no longer needed mothering, but she and her aunt had known one another for longer than she had known her own mother. If she did need mothering at any time Daphne could be relied upon to play that role impeccably.

The two sisters were unalike in what they had wanted from life. Alex's mother had married a farmer, and it had seemed to Alex that money nearly always seemed to be on the verge of running out. Her father hated spending anything and pretended to be hard up even when the farm was doing well. Her mother loved being a farmer's wife, adored the countryside and would not have changed her lifestyle for anything. Daphne was the opposite. She had married an art dealer whose collection of old masters, too valuable to be kept at home, was housed in a gallery in Paris, which he also owned. Although their main home was in London, their winters were spent either on their yacht in the Caribbean or in a villa in St Moritz. They had no children. Daphne loved Alex and loved entertaining. She had given her niece the keys to her London home years before and begged her to use it, to stay in it or to entertain in it. It would give the staff something to do. Alex had taken her up only when there had been something to celebrate. Calling her aunt on her mobile elicited an unequivocal yes from Mustique, followed by the instruction to 'Put everything on my account at Harrods. I'll call and give them the OK.'

It was not without trepidation that Alex told the group it was near enough to her birthday and this time lunch was on her. Although it was not strictly true Lola looked at her friend. She wanted to say, 'Who are you trying to impress', but she knew the answer.

Drago said, 'I'll do drinks.'

Luc offered to cook, saying, 'If there's a kitchen I could do scaloppini di Milano with some pasta and a fried egg on it.'

Alex said, 'I want it to be a surprise lunch, because it might be our last chance.'

She did not say for what and no one asked her. Alex thanked them for their offers but told them that she wanted to do it herself before they went on their travels. When she got home she telephoned Silas.

TWENTY-NINE

Silas had now made three calls to Luc without anything that he had hoped for happening. He had come to the conclusion that Luc seemed not to be too happy on the phone and wondered whether email might be a better option. There had been one call from Benedict who, feeling guilty for being so short with him in the park, had asked when he would be coming back to the gym. Silas had replied with a tentative 'never'. Refusing to take 'never' for an answer Benedict had walked around to his place that evening and took a surprised Silas to the pub. Awkward silences had punctuated the meeting, but in the event nothing had come of it. Silas was left wondering how he could return to the group whose company he missed without losing face. The last person he expected to hear from was Alex.

'How are things, Silas?' She made her voice sound more welcoming than she felt.

It was not until he replied 'I'm good, thanks' that she remembered why she had called him.

Blushing, she was glad he could not see her. She wanted him to be at Daphne's so that he could see what background she came from. She wanted him to regret that she was no longer interested in him and hoped that he would realize how foolish he had been to give her up – although it was she who had terminated their relationship. Nothing of this occurred to Silas. As soon as Alex said it was her birthday and her turn to invite the group to lunch, he thought of it only as a good way to get together with his friends again. He did not want to be thought of as someone who never missed an opportunity to miss an opportunity. It was not as if he was pleading with them to allow him back. It was because he had been invited, not to the gym to which he was free to return but to lunch.

'Twelve o' clock at the gym next Wednesday?' Alex said

'I'll be there.'

Silas tried to make it sound as if the weeks in the wilderness had not happened because they had not happened for him. His gym attendance had not disappeared without trace. He had always known the option to reinstate it was there, but until that moment something had put it on hold.

None the less it was a strange experience for him as, when Wednesday came around, he anxiously approached his friends. They sat chatting, waiting to head off for Alex's lunch, everyone pretending they had not noticed he had not been seen for weeks or that his absence had been the subject of discussion. They greeted him as if nothing had happened but felt a certain awkwardness. A conversation they associated with the other group took place, and for the few minutes they seemed to have become merely acquaintances. They discussed the weather, the buses and the *Strictly Come Dancing* show which had been on television the previous evening. Minds froze, intimacy vanished, a spell was broken and the magic that buoyed the group was no longer there. It was as if a cold draught had blown in with Silas. They were facing a challenge. At Benedict's lunch they had managed to adapt to being outside their comfort zone, although they were still dependent on being together. They had even adapted to having the two women join them by pretending they were pseudo-males. Now they were faced with having to adapt to a renegade, a non-believer, a suicide bomber, to someone who had decided that he no longer acknowledged what they stood for and claimed actively to despise it.

The girls were not with them. They assumed that they would be at Alex's aunt's home preparing the lunch. Where else could they be? Their presence might have helped. They needed them. It would have lightened the atmosphere. Alex and Lola were components of their group, and they had come to accept them. They might have diluted the negative influence Silas seemed to have brought in with him.

Luc stood up. 'Time to make a move.'

Things were different. They were going out for lunch but looked as if they were going to a funeral. They tried not to feel apprehensive. Was it because having women deal with lunch reminded them of home and adult responsibility, something from which the gym allowed a respectable escape? Whatever it was, they let their feet do their thinking and found themselves once again on the pavement outside the gym. This time they knew where they were going. Alex had given them Daphne's address, and a feeling of pleasurable anticipation began to be felt as once again they gathered together into the entity they believed themselves to be and with which they were familiar.

Sitting in two taxis that past experience had told them they needed, they found themselves in areas of London none of them recognized. They wondered whether Daphne had a garden. The weather was too pleasant to be indoors. With an image in their minds of Benedict greeting them with a saucepan in one hand and a teacloth in the other, they waited for the taxis to deliver them to the next stage of their journey. No further thought was needed.

They were surprised when the front door was opened by a butler who led them through a large hall, past glimpses of large rooms to the garden where Alex and Lola, one in *grande dame* role and the other looking mildly worried, stood waiting. On a large terrace several small tables were covered with white table-cloths on which salvers of canapés had been laid out. Alex and Lola in summer dresses greeted them, and the group had a few moments to adapt to a new setting with which their collective memory was unable to identify. Their first impression was of Alex and Lola dressed in unfamiliar clothes, and their second impression was their inability to work out where they were. As they struggled to get their bearings they could not help but notice that on this occasion the lunch was in a league that none of them had expected. Aunt Daphne's home and garden would not have looked out of place in a glossy magazine. A glass of Veuve Clicquot in their not unwilling hands, they were led by the girls towards a table on a well-kept lawn where a buffet lunch was imaginatively displayed on a pale-green tablecloth.

'Blimey,' Harold said, while Corker murmured, 'Looks like *Midsummer Night's Dream*.'

Quail's eggs and spring rolls were passed around as they admired the shrubbery that shielded them from the faint hum of traffic as well as the flowerbeds that were obviously tended by professionals. They wandered around the tennis court, the green-house and the grape vines, while their hostess played the *châtelaine* and became increasingly anxious. She had achieved what she had set out to do but was having trouble thinking exactly what it was. After their initial surprise, no one seemed particularly impressed with the scene she had set up. Within moments they had adapted to the surroundings and were engaging in their usual abstractions. Alex noticed something she had not picked up on before. The group, all of whom were very much older than she, were enjoying themselves in the spirit of play. In the grandiose and unfamiliar surroundings their capacity for enjoyment had not deserted them. It was what kept them together in the gym and elsewhere. Silas had taken it all too seriously. He didn't want to play games. Unlike the others he was avoiding the experience of a second childhood because he had as yet not dealt appropriately with his first.

Alex felt alone. She belonged neither at Daphne's mansion nor in the group. She was unready. Life was before her not behind her. She had no idea what to do next. Her journey was just beginning, and she did not know where it would take her. She knew only that she must set out soon, with or without Lola. The group may not have been a therapy group, as Harold had thought, but it had certainly been therapeutic, and she had learned a great deal from it. Having an affair with Benedict, who had continued to be on her mind, would take her nowhere other than back to where she had started. Would having an affair with Lola be any different?

She was on a race track, an Indy 500 driver going round and round in circles going nowhere fast. She wanted to get off. She was no longer interested in the fruits of victory, neither was she impressed with ejaculatory champagne bottles. She realized why women did not go in for circuit racing. She wanted neither to spray champagne over her team's supporters nor over Daphne's dress which she had borrowed.

She was becoming increasingly frightened and speechless and gulped down her champagne to prevent her from spilling it. Benedict was talking animatedly to some of the group, but in the surroundings she had created she was having difficulty in recognizing them. She scarcely saw them, hoping that they would not see her, wishing herself invisible, wishing she could pull something over her head. She was sweating, her heart was thumping. She needed to sit down until it was time to leave. She was scarcely aware of Benedict who had not spoken to her since his arrival. Only a few minutes had passed, although to Alex it seemed much longer.

'Your aunt has a lovely home.'

She blushed. He was expecting her to contribute to the conversation. She could think of nothing to say. 'I'm not too keen on parties.'

Benedict was about to follow this up with something witty, but nothing came to mind. He was running out of things to say, and Alex knew she had to make conversation. She had to talk to someone. She had desperately wanted to talk to Benedict, but when it came to it she had nothing to say. She was back at a local farmer's party to which her father had taken her when she was sixteen. The occasion was so clear in her mind that it was as if she actually were there and once again having to make conversation with strangers. She remembered being embarrassed, not least because her father had shown her off to other men as if she were his possession, boasting to them of her beauty, her talents and her achievements at school. She had wondered at the time whether he wanted to give the impression that she was less a daughter than a girlfriend. Did he hope that other men would envy him? She recalled that her father's behaviour was often too much to take and remembered that more than once she had found herself vomiting in the toilet. At the time she knew that she was not ill, only sick of his behaviour. She was so self-conscious that she had wished she had been wearing dark glasses, so that she could delude herself that if she were to look through a glass darkly strange men would not be able to see her.

Her past had come back to haunt her. Anxieties she had had as an adolescent were resurfacing. She was out of her depth. She might be in Daphne's garden, but she was no longer an adult. She felt as embarrassed as a teenager and recalled why she had been so afraid to show her face. Convincing herself that her father had become too close physically, she had done nothing to prevent it, and everyone would be able to see that that was what had happened. For a long time after that she had been terrified in social situations. Unwilling to allow anyone to see what she believed to be her wicked past she tried to remind herself where she was but only partly succeeded.

'Makes a nice change from exercising the horses,' she heard herself say – to her horror.

Benedict wondered why she was talking about horses and put it down to not having paid enough attention to the conversation. There might be a lot more to Alex than he had thought.

Becoming less self-conscious by the minute, Alex thanked God for champagne. Someone came past with a bottle and topped up their glasses, and she knew that as long as she continued to drink she might be able to get through the lunch without disaster.

'What about something to eat?' she suggested to Benedict.

Most of them had already helped themselves and had rearranged the garden chairs to suit them. She was as struck by the lavishness of the food Daphne had provided as presumably, she assumed, the rest of the group must have been. She realized that everything was either pink or green. Salmon and lobster, smoked ham and green salad, pink champagne, strawberries and wild raspberries. Long green stems of pink gladioli and pale-green plates. The garden, the food and drink and the catering made it look as if a reception was taking place. Daphne meant well, but it might well take her a very long time to live down. It's fortunate, she thought, that we'll be going away soon. Alex took a little of everything, her curiosity overriding her concerns. She was beginning to enjoy herself. Taking their plates over to an oak tree and sitting beneath its shade, she and Benedict began their picnic. She was starting to enjoy the afternoon, and the others seemed to be enjoying it, too. The Veuve Cliquot helped. It was turning out exactly as she had planned it.

She saw her life stretching out before her. There had been the beginning. That was over. Lola and Silas had helped her come to terms with what had gone wrong with it. The next stage was about to begin. She was not frightened. She was looking forward to it. She felt more equipped to deal with it. She knew that much of her strength had come not so much from the gym but from the group. She would try to put the past behind her. Of all of them her past was probably the most traumatic, but, with a bit of luck, her future could be the most fulfilling. She looked around the garden. She was happy with what she had done. Her gym friends were eating and drinking but, as usual, mostly talking. The lunch had gone off well. Her swan song had come to an end.

THIRTY

The group's acceptance of the past and its effect on the here and now was about to be confronted. In the week after Alex's birthday lunch they had all arrived more or less at the same time and waited for someone to start the usual debate. Alex's lunch would be on the agenda.

The lunch had been more than just a lunch. It had been a statement. They needed to talk about it. Was it a milestone, a signal, a message? No one knew quite what it was. They waited to find out. But for a while no one spoke.

It was not that no one had anything to say about it but that everyone had an opinion. No one wanted to be the first in case he had failed to read the signs correctly. It was Harold, who had the greatest need to withhold information, who was the first to speak. He was feeling good about himself and felt that he had acquired a standing in the group that he had previously not had. Perhaps he had been given it earlier, but he had not taken it up. It had to do with belonging, a feeling of being at home, of acceptance. It had to do with the lunch. He felt relaxed and briefly wondered why he was not thinking of what usually worried him. He was standing before his peers at the Oxford Union, at the dispatch box in the House of Commons, at the General Assembly of the United Nations. He resumed his seat before his grandiosity overwhelmed him.

'I have to say' – his tone was appropriate to his self-appointed status – 'it was good of Aunt Daphne to provide the location for Alex's birthday lunch. We've had two lunches. Both of them were amazing. I think it would be not just difficult but impossible for any of us to host another as brilliantly as Alex did this one. I certainly couldn't.' He looked around as if challenging someone to contradict him. Having delivered this information, which no one felt the need to dispute and with which they were all familiar, he paused to gather his thoughts. They waited while he did so. Harold was beginning to wonder why he was addressing them so solemnly. He had begun in that mode and was finding it difficult to modify it. Perhaps Aunt Daphne's palatial home had something to do with it. He was good at taking on the colouring of his surroundings. What he was not good at was being himself.

He coughed and continued. 'Alex is not here, so we can't tell her how much we enjoyed it. I'm sure she must know that anyway. What I liked was that it was private. We were not overlooked or overheard. We were in our own world. Privacy is important. Did we need it? Was it because we wanted to merge into the background in case we stuck out like a sore thumb?' He realized it was not a sore thumb he meant. He looked around shiftily to see if anyone had realized what he was referring to and managed to gather himself together again. 'We are usually so unaware of our surroundings that we are able to concentrate entirely on ourselves. We lost that for a moment or two when we arrived. But within a short time, *where* we were faded into the background and *why* we were resurfaced.'

Why was he emphasizing what they all knew? He wished he was standing at a reading desk in a lecture theatre, and then he would have written his thoughts down and carefully edited them. He had forgotten that he was a phoney person who had never actually given a lecture. He wished that he could say as others could, 'I am who I am, rather than I am who I'm not. There was something about the lunch that made the day special but, despite that, or perhaps because of it, "why we were" actually did take over from "where we were".' What he actually did say was, 'Our surroundings infected us with its harmony. There are thoughts and ideas and activities that we keep to ourselves. They range from opinions that might be hurtful to some aspects of biology.'

He had not intended to mention biology. He wished he could forget about biology for a bit. He hoped no one wondered to what he was referring. 'In the garden we were having an anything-goes experience, a mirror image of our collective thoughts and feelings. We've had that before. In the Chinese restaurant we ceased to be individuals and became a cohesive group. It happened again at Benedict's studio. I know the surroundings were different, but in the gym we have learned to bother only with the here and now. In Daphne's garden we became a presence again. An all-for-one and a one-for-all presence.' He wished he had left that last bit out. Too pretentious. No one seemed either to notice or understand what he was saying.

Harold was making a point that he knew to be important, but why it was important he was not entirely sure. Was he thinking of revealing his secret? Was he afraid it might pop out? He quickly went on to say, 'It is what we have come to expect from the gym, and although it was in a different location it felt the same. In other words we feel at one with one another wherever we are. Some of us were worried about that. Nothing changed after Benedict's lunch, and nothing changed this time either. I also liked the fact that nothing was left to chance. Everything was taken care of. It's rare for that to happen. We have all expected things to go wrong in our lives, and suddenly we find ourselves in a situation where nothing does,' he ended lamely.

There were murmurings of approval. Harold had something else to say but would keep it to himself. He realized that he had not only found his voice but he had also found his maleness. His maleness was who he was, his right to be whoever he was capable of being. He could stand up for himself as well as the next man. He need no longer pretend to be what he was not.

Jerry had also worked out why they felt as they did. He said, 'I agree with Harold. It's not that we didn't like Daphne's garden, or even that we did like it, or that we found ourselves in a different location. We've always known that where we are, or who we are – we didn't know who we were for a very long time – is not as important as why we are. We may still not be sure as to why we are, although I think we are closer to finding out. We are in "why we are" mode at Alex's or Benedict's or any restaurant or café we happen to be in. Preferably at a round table. The feeling of enclosure not only makes us feel safe but seems to remind us of much earlier enclosures in which we did not feel safe at all. We like thinking about why we are. Sometimes we can only understand it clearly if we stand back from it.'

He was taking a sideways swipe at Silas who was listening and for once not thinking 'What a Wally!' as he invariably did before his age of enlightenment set in. He stopped speaking when he realized that he had still not told any of them about his embarrassingly awful mother.

Luc said, 'I'm still not sure about the "why we are" business.'

'It's a question we ask ourselves from time to time,' replied Jerry. 'We have only recently discovered why we enjoy being together. We all get something out of it, but it may not be the same thing for everyone. It could be.'

Drago asked, 'Do you mean in the group we feel something special to each of us?'

'Yes. What we find is what we are looking for. How I see it is this. We are born with an entitlement. It is essentially to be cared for and as a result to be free to evolve in any direction that our talents and abilities take us. We're unique. Every creature through-out the animal kingdom has that right.'

'The problem is that we are entitled to be angry in the absence of it as long as we don't take out our anger on other people, which is what many do,' Benedict pointed out. 'Some of us have turned our swords into ploughshares or switched to competitive sport. I was thinking of darts and archery. They were missiles once but toys now.'

It was obvious now to Benedict why Jerry enjoyed coming. He's never given up asking why. Y is a crooked letter might have been the right answer for him. He's in his element discovering what's going on. He's been playing the detective all his life. He would prob-ably have been one even if his father hadn't succeeded in turning his life into a detective story. No one minds that. They like having someone showing an interest in them. If Jerry had not met us he would most likely be having a miserable retirement sitting at home doing cryptic crosswords, and we would probably still be coming to the gym but not to the brain gym. We would be exchanging small talk while we are on the machines like the others do. It's done us all good. No one needs to ask questions any more because they already know the answers. And it doesn't matter where we are so long as we're together. We could be over at Franco's having a sandwich or even, say, holidaying in a rented house at the seaside for a week.

Jerry was thinking of something else. 'The group obviously provides us with an interest. We talk about issues, we offer our slant on what's going on in the world, and we relax after exercise rather than rushing in, working out and rushing back. We don't go back to work because we don't have any work. Our time is our own. We were lonelier than we realized, and life had ceased to be as enjoy-able and as intellectually rewarding as we now know it can be. Most of what we all did before, we did on our own. We worked on our own. Some of us had no one to play with, so we played on our own. There's nothing wrong with that, but we've discovered it's better when other people are involved. It may have been slightly different for Silas because there were people in his life. He used models for his bronzes. But Benedict needed only a ruler and a pencil, Corker sat at home with *Macbeth*, Luc used to cook only for himself and Drago conducted orchestras while listening to the radio. No women were needed. We made a tacit decision to be an all-male group. We did not want to share our feelings with women. We had good reasons for this. Our mothers had not shared their feelings with us. They had not understood our needs. We spoke of abandonment, of neglect and the need some of us had to treat women as scapegoats. Then we moved on and benefited from having Alex and Lola join us.'

'But what strikes me most,' said Benedict, 'is that we have discovered how to be happy again. The joy of being, of not having to do anything responsible, the joy of a second childhood. We've needed second childhoods because our first were not as they should have been. We laugh. Even Silas, whose aim was to grow up and take life more seriously, wanted to play games. He was a practical joker. To begin with, he could only laugh when someone was discomfited. It was apple-pie-bed humour, scapegoating humour not real humour. He was angry then, but he's changed. He would never have recognized the need for change had it not been for the group.'

'There is another thing,' said Drago. 'Before I came to the gym I am with my computer. All the time I am doing the networking. I don't need friends now to follow me on Twitter or talk to me on Facebook. I am in contact with someone every minute. Now I have real friends. To have access is good, numbers are good, plural is good, but few is better. You do not love the many, only the one. Do I need 800 million friends? I don't think so. Face to face has to be better than face to book.'

There was silence for a while. Then Corker spoke, for the first time with his own voice. They found themselves listening to Corker's thoughts rather than Shakespeare's. 'What pleases me most is that I have been able not just to be like a child but to feel like a child. Some of the feelings were painful, but others were wonderful. It has helped me to have another look at what my life was like when I was growing up. It was not perfect, but it was not terrible. I turned to acting not to look for admiration or to be pleasing to others but because I needed to be in another world where I was able to speak not only when I was spoken to, but even when no one spoke to me. But they were not my words. They were the words in the script. I did not have any words of my own. I never spoke up for myself, and if I did no one listened or I was told to be quiet. Later on I spoke so quietly that no one could hear me. I learned how to be someone else. I was whoever I wanted to be. I was a chameleon. In the gym I was a gymnast, on the bus I was a fragile old man who needed a seat, at home I was the wallpaper. In *Macbeth* I was part of a conversation. I felt at home with *Macbeth* because it was violent. My parents did their best. They seldom hit me physically, but they often hit me verbally. I can let go now. I couldn't before. I hung on to them because I thought they still owed me something. Well, whatever they may have owed me they won't be giving it to me now.'

'Seek and you shall find,' said Jerry. 'It's all in the Bible somewhere.'

'Does that mean,' asked Drago, 'that what we are looking for is there somewhere if we know what we look for? Because that is what Corker says has happened to him.' Answering his own question he said. 'I think that the more we stay angry we will not find what we look for. Anger and love do not go together. What we find in the gym is contentment.'

'Biblical sermons are all very well,' said Benedict, 'but if there is no one listening it's not a sermon.'

'And if no one can hear you,' remarked Corker, 'it's as if you haven't spoken.'

Silas contributed, 'And if you don't know who you're supposed to be talking to you end up talking to yourself.'

'When I was at school,' said Benedict, 'what I remember most clearly was the teacher telling us that it was forbidden to speak in class. If we broke that rule we had to write out fifty times, "Silence is golden. Only monkeys chatter." A terrible thing to impress upon a child. It's taken me a long time to realize that it's speaking that's golden. Silence is hostile. Give someone the cold shoulder, and the next thing is you are thinking of hitting him before he hits you. Monkeys do chatter. I'd like to think that they listen as well. Jerry once said that what we do is not as important as why we do.'

Jerry mused over this. 'I've always thought that "why" is more important than "what" or "when".' He remembered suddenly how 'why' had become so important. It was his father's refusal to answer his questions or at best only reply cryptically. It was what had got him where he was. A detective superintendent was not bad, but what about his masters in psychotherapy which he had achieved after he had retired, when most people he knew sat at home watching television all day and boasting that they would not dream of learning how to use a mobile phone, never mind a computer. If anyone wanted to get in touch with them they could telephone. What with his irritating father and his distant mother, not to mention his Victorian nanny, it was surprising that he had managed to grow up at all.

'Why are you sighing'? Harold asked.

'I've been going over in my mind,' Jerry replied, 'my childhood, and I suddenly realized that, however disappointing it may have been and however much I've blamed my parents, in the event I've not done too badly. I've learned a lot from constantly questioning everything.'

Harold felt himself becoming anxious. 'You're all talking about yourselves.' They like themselves, he thought. Everyone is trying to understand why we get on so well. I've always hated myself. Well, at least a part of myself. Do I still want to turn my back on everyone? He thought of how much he had changed. He was much more open now. After all, it can't be so terrible to look male. Half the world does. The bottom line was that he needed people, and he was relieved that people needed him. It was time he faced the other way.

Silas wanted to speak, but he had said it all.

Luc was about to say, 'We'd better be making a move', when Alex and Lola arrived.

'We've come to say goodbye,' said Alex. They looked like the two young women they were. Why had they been part of the group? No one could remember.

'We're off to Australia tomorrow. We'll bump into you all again one day.'

Corker waved goodbye. He was about to say, 'Look not on the order of your going' but amended it to 'Look after yourselves.'

The girls regarded their friends. It was time to go.

SOME AUTHORS WE HAVE PUBLISHED

James Agee • Bella Akhmadulina • Tariq Ali • Kenneth Allsop

Alfred Andersch • Guillaume Apollinaire • Machado de Assis • Miguel Angel Asturias

Duke of Bedford • Oliver Bernard • Thomas Blackburn • Jane Bowles • Paul Bowles

Richard Bradford • Ilse, Countess von Bredow • Lenny Bruce • Finn Carling

Blaise Cendrars • Marc Chagall • Giorgio de Chirico • Uno Chiyo • Hugo Claus

Jean Cocteau • Albert Cohen • Colette • Ithell Colquhoun • Richard Corson

Benedetto Croce • Margaret Crosland • e.e. cummings • Stig Dalager • Salvador Dalí

Osamu Dazai • Anita Desai • Charles Dickens • Fabián Dobles • William Donaldson

Autran Dourado • Yuri Druzhnikov • Lawrence Durrell • Isabelle Eberhardt

Sergei Eisenstein • Shusaku Endo • Erté • Knut Faldbakken • Ida Fink

Wolfgang George Fischer • Nicholas Freeling • Philip Freund • Carlo Emilio Gadda

Rhea Galanaki • Salvador Garmendia • Michel Gauquelin • André Gide

Natalia Ginzburg • Jean Giono • Geoffrey Gorer • William Goyen • Julien Gracq

Sue Grafton • Robert Graves • Angela Green • Julien Green • George Grosz

Barbara Hardy • H.D. • Rayner Heppenstall • David Herbert • Gustaw Herling

Hermann Hesse • Shere Hite • Stewart Home • Abdullah Hussein

King Hussein of Jordan • Ruth Inglis • Grace Ingoldby • Yasushi Inoue

Hans Henny Jahnn • Karl Jaspers • Takeshi Kaiko • Jaan Kaplinski • Anna Kavan

Yasunuri Kawabata • Nikos Kazantzakis • Orhan Kemal • Christer Kihlman

James Kirkup • Paul Klee • James Laughlin • Patricia Laurent • Violette Leduc

Lee Seung-U • Vernon Lee • József Lengyel • Robert Liddell • Francisco García Lorca

Moura Lympany • Dacia Maraini • Marcel Marceau • André Maurois • Henri Michaux

Henry Miller • Miranda Miller • Marga Minco • Yukio Mishima • Quim Monzó

Margaret Morris • Angus Wolfe Murray • Atle Næss • Gérard de Nerval • Anaïs Nin

Yoko Ono • Uri Orlev • Wendy Owen • Arto Paasilinna • Marco Pallis • Oscar Parland

Boris Pasternak • Cesare Pavese • Milorad Pavic • Octaviò Paz • Mervyn Peake

Carlos Pedretti • Dame Margery Perham • Graciliano Ramos • Jeremy Reed

Rodrigo Rey Rosa • Joseph Roth • Ken Russell • Marquis de Sade • Cora Sandel

George Santayana • May Sarton • Jean-Paul Sartre • Ferdinand de Saussure

Gerald Scarfe • Albert Schweitzer • George Bernard Shaw • Isaac Bashevis Singer

Patwant Singh • Edith Sitwell • Suzanne St Albans • Stevie Smith

C.P. Snow • Bengt Söderbergh • Vladimir Soloukhin • Natsume Soseki

Muriel Spark Gertrude Stein • Bram Stoker • August Strindberg

Rabindranath Tagore • Tambimuttu • Elisabeth Russell Taylor • Anne Tibble

Roland Topor • Miloš Urban • Anne Valery • Peter Vansittart • José J. Veiga

Tarjei Vesaas • Noel Virtue • Max Weber • Edith Wharton • William Carlos Williams

Phyllis Willmott • G. Peter Winnington • Monique Wittig • A.B. Yehoshua

Marguerite Young • Fakhar Zaman • Alexander Zinoviev • Emile Zola